The LAKE *in the* CLOUDS

A **free** eBook edition is available
with the purchase of this print book.

The LAKE in the CLOUDS

EDWARD WILLETT

© Edward Willett, 2015

Edited by Matthew Hughes
Cover and text designed by Tania Craan
Typeset by Susan Buck
Printed and bound in Canada at Friesens

Library and Archives Canada Cataloguing in Publication
Willett, Edward, 1959-, author
   The lake in the clouds / Edward Willett.
(The shards of Excalibur ; book 3)
Issued in print and electronic formats.
ISBN 978-1-55050-616-7 (pbk.).--ISBN 978-1-55050-617-4 (pdf).--
ISBN 978-1-55050-823-9 (epub).--ISBN 978-1-55050-824-6 (mobi)

      I. Title. II. Series: Willett, Edward, 1959- . The shards of
Excalibur ; book 3

PS8595.I5424L33 2015   jC813'.54   C2014-908234-7

Library of Congress Control Number: 2014956826

2517 Victoria Avenue
Regina, Saskatchewan
Canada S4P 0T2
www.coteaubooks.com

10 9 8 7 6 5 4 3 2 1

Available in Canada from:
Publishers Group Canada
2440 Viking Way
Richmond, British Columbia
Canada V6V 1N2

Available in the US from:
Orca Book Publishers
www.orcabook.com
1-800-210-5277

Coteau Books gratefully acknowledges the financial support of its publishing program by: the Saskatchewan Arts Board, The Canada Council for the Arts, the Government of Canada through the Canada Book Fund and the Government of Saskatchewan through the Creative Industry Growth and Sustainability program of the Ministry of Parks, Culture and Sport.

Four nieces and a nephew – five books
This one is for Torrey

CHAPTER ONE

FAIRY ISLAND

ARIANE AWOKE TO THE *putt-putt-putt* of an outboard motor.

Jerked out of a dream she couldn't quite remember – there had been mountains, water, and of course Excalibur, which was *always* in her dreams – she blinked up at the underside of the bunk over her head for a moment before memory kicked in and she rolled over in her sleeping bag, all at once, and peered out through the tiny opening in the curtains that was all she dared allow herself.

It was the same old-fashioned aluminum boat she'd seen three times the day before. In the pre-dawn twilight, it was nosing along the shore of the mainland, just a couple of hundred metres across the waters of Emma Lake. A man sat in the stern, hand on the throttle, intently studying the nearest cabin on that side of the water: Aunt Phyllis's cabin.

Ariane had decided not to rejoin Aunt Phyllis, but she hadn't gone far. Worn out from the journey across the Atlantic, hurting and angry from Wally's betrayal – he'd chosen to join forces with Merlin and give the ancient sorcerer the shard of Excalibur Ariane had retrieved from the cave in France – she'd slipped into the water of Emma

Lake but travelled no farther than the eerily appropriately named Fairy Island, where a summer cabin stood directly opposite Aunt Phyllis's, locked and shuttered for the season. She'd broken in by fashioning a spear of ice to smash the lock. She'd eaten cold canned chili and corn chips, drunk bottled water, stripped off her dirty clothes, and wrapped herself in one of the sleeping bags rolled up in the bunk beds in a tiny bedroom off the combined kitchen/living room that took up most of the space. She'd spent the whole next day in the chilly cabin, much of it staring at the phone, wondering if she should call her aunt.

That had been three days ago. In the ensuing time she'd eaten just about everything left in the cabin. She'd found a stack of books, every single one of them by Danielle Steel, and had read two that were bestsellers (though she couldn't see why), ten years before she was born. She'd napped. She'd waited, and waited, and *waited*, hoping the third shard of Excalibur would make its presence known.

It hadn't. And she still hadn't made up her mind whether or not to phone Aunt Phyllis.

She'd watched her mother's sister leave the cabin every day, walking away down the road on the other side and coming back an hour later. Her "morning constitutional," her aunt called it. At night she'd seen her through the cabin windows, eating a lonely supper, reading. Once or twice she'd seen her use the telephone. *Trying to find out what happened to me?* Ariane wondered. She felt guilty. But she still didn't call.

And then yesterday morning the boat with its tiny outboard motor had chugged past for the first time. A few hours later it had chugged past again. And once more, just at twilight. It had disappeared down the lake to the east, where most of the cabins were, as night had closed in, but here it was back again. And the man in it didn't *only* watch Aunt Phyllis's cabin. Part of the time he focused his attention on the cabin where Ariane hid.

It was the sole structure remaining on Fairy Island, except for the historic cabin of the artist Ernest Lindner at the northwest tip, and dated to the same era: the 1930s. Ariane had often wondered how it had survived. Certainly, no new construction was allowed on the island, which she'd always understood was a wildlife refuge. But through whatever quirk of history, here it was, and here she was, with a view of Aunt Phyllis's cabin – and the boatman with an unusual interest in it.

He has to be one of Rex Major's people, Ariane thought. *Keeping an eye on Aunt Phyllis. But is he really interested in her, or is he waiting for* me *to show up?*

She rolled away from the window and lay staring up at the top bunk, feeling almost physically ill. Four days since returning from France, and she still hadn't decided what to do.

She'd thought, when she'd first decided not to return to Aunt Phyllis, that she would simply rest for a few hours until her strength returned, then sense the location of the third shard and go to retrieve it. But though she'd done nothing but rest since then, still she sensed nothing. And she didn't even know enough about the magic to know what that absence of the third shard's song meant. Was the shard hidden away from water? Was it on the other side of the planet? Had it been destroyed?

She didn't think the latter was likely. The sword wasn't an ordinary sword, and she doubted it could be destroyed like an ordinary piece of steel: melted down and made into rivets or whatever. But the first two shards had both been hidden in water, or very close to it. If a shard had been moved away from water...would she still sense it? Her power – the power of the Lady of the Lake – was so intimately bound up with water she wasn't at all certain.

Or was something else going on?

She remembered her flight across the Atlantic, how she had reached for the power of the first shard – then strapped to her belly, now lying under her pillow – and failed to find it. Could the fact Merlin had the second shard – *the one Wally gave him,* she thought bitterly – be interfering with her ability to sense the third?

And if so, what could she do about it?

She didn't know. Didn't have a clue. And didn't have anyone she could talk to. Aunt Phyllis wouldn't be able to advise her, and if Ariane contacted her she might very well be putting her aunt in danger. Wally had abandoned her. The Lady of the Lake – who had shown up, uninvited, in Wascana Lake in Regina to proclaim Ariane her heir and give her some of the Lady's power so she could take up the quest to find the shards of Excalibur – had been banished from Earth by Merlin before she was quite done talking. Apparently the door from Earth to Faerie was not completely blocked, or all magic would have vanished: but Ariane did not know how to access it, or how to reach through it to the Lady.

And here I am on Fairy Island, she thought. *You'd think it would be some help.*

She got up, but didn't get dressed – she couldn't bear to put on her filthy clothes unless she had to. Instead she unzipped the sleeping bag completely and then draped it around herself like a thick cloak. She went into the kitchen and opened the cupboard. There was nothing left in there now but a box of salt, a few cans of tuna fish, and a big package of stale tortilla chips. She'd drunk the last of the bottled water the owners had left behind the day before.

She opened one of the cans of tuna, spread its contents on half a dozen of the tortilla chips, ate, licked her fingers, and then, with a sigh, set about getting dressed. She needed to go to the toilet, and that meant going outside, slipping along the path behind the cabin to the outhouse fifteen metres away among the trees. Before she risked it, she took a careful look through all the windows for any signs of life on the lake. The cabin would hide her from anyone across the channel, including Aunt Phyllis, but not from anyone in a boat in the right place. The coast seemed clear, so she slipped out, did what she needed to do, and then opened the outhouse door...only to hear the *putt-putt-putt* of the outboard motor again.

And this time, it was nosing along *her* shore.

She pulled the outhouse door almost closed and listened. *Go on by*, she thought. *Go on by, go on by...*

But instead, the motor changed tone, then stopped. She heard footsteps on wooden planks. The man had landed on the little floating dock. He was coming up to the cabin.

And she'd left the door open.

Does he know I'm here? she thought. *Is he planning to grab me and take me back to Rex Major?*

Not while I have a whole lake to draw on, he won't.

Then she had an even greater shock: she heard two voices, a man *and* a woman. She pushed the door to the outhouse open just a little farther, mostly so she could hear better, but also so she could get a breath of fresher air, and heard, "...built in 1933...only building on the island except for the Ernest Lindner cabin...wildlife refuge...grandfathered...has to be torn down once the current owner dies..." The woman seemed to be giving the man a tour of the place. Then her voice changed. "Someone's broken in!"

Ariane swore to herself.

The voices vanished. She guessed they were inside. She thought about making a break for it, running for the water. She could plunge into it and disappear before they could do anything.

But she didn't dare. If the man really was one of Rex Major's minions, he would immediately realize who she was. And tell Major she had successfully made it back from France. Right now Major had to be wondering if she had simply vanished over the Atlantic. As long as she wasn't spotted, he would *keep* wondering. The minute he knew she was back in Canada, he might grab Aunt Phyllis as a hostage.

And then her heart leaped to her throat. There was another very good reason she couldn't simply flee into the water: *she had left the first shard of Excalibur underneath the pillow of the bottom bunk bed.* All it would take was for Major's man to lift that pillow, trying to figure out who had spent the night in the cabin...

Pulse pounding in her ears, she stood in the outhouse, and waited.

The back door she had come out of just minutes earlier opened. She let the outhouse door close almost all the way.

"No one here now," the man was saying. "Looks like they just spent the night and then took off. A tramp, maybe?"

"Maybe," the woman said. "Although a tramp with a boat is kind of odd. And we don't get a lot of homeless people up here." Her voice brightened. "Well, a bit of a mystery, but never mind that. What do you think of the place?"

"It should do me fine," the man said. "It has just the view I was looking for."

"Really?" the woman said. She sounded doubtful. "You can't see much but the cabins on the lakeshore over there."

"Not the cabin," the man said smoothly. "The island. I'm an artist. Planning to paint all winter."

"Well, this is certainly the place for that," the woman said. "Emma Lake is quite famous among Canadian artists. But you know that. That's why you're here."

"Absolutely," the man said. Even if she hadn't known he was lying, Ariane would have known he was lying, just from the way he said it. But the real estate lady – as she presumed the woman to be – either didn't notice or didn't care.

"Well, then," she said. "If you'll take me back across, we'll go into town and sign the papers."

"Just a minute," the man said, and to Ariane's horror, she heard footsteps on the wooden steps of the back porch, and then on the path leading to the outhouse. *Just my luck,* she thought, *he has to pee.* She readied herself for a frantic dash into the cottage. She'd have to grab the shard and then somehow get to the lake...

But the steps didn't come as far as the outhouse. They stopped. She held her breath, for more reasons than one, and waited. And waited. Just when she thought she'd have to breathe or pass out, the steps resumed...and went away from her. "All right," the man said. "Let's head back. It's perfect."

The voices faded around to the other side of the cabin. Ariane opened the door and looked out. Footsteps on the dock...and then the *putt-putt-putt* of the outboard.

"Going back to town" probably meant going all the way to Prince Albert, almost fifty kilometres away. The man would be gone for at least a couple of hours.

Ariane didn't mean to waste that time.

For the moment, Aunt Phyllis's cabin wasn't being watched.

She went back inside the cabin. She went first to the bunk. Her pillow was undisturbed, and the first shard of Excalibur, the sharp point and a few inches of pitted steel – if it was steel – was still where she had foolishly left it, wrapped in a tensor bandage. She pulled up her dirty T-shirt and wrapped the shard tight to her skin again. Then she tugged her shirt down and picked up the phone.

It was an old rotary-dial model, and she was sure it was a landline: she'd looked outside and traced the wires to where they disappeared into the lake, presumably running along the lake bed. It seemed unlikely it came anywhere near the Internet, which was a good thing, since Rex Major's – Merlin's – software ran much of the Internet and was infused with a tiny amount of magic, allowing him to… well, she and Wally had never been entirely sure *what* it allowed him to do – except for little things like bringing a computer-game monster to life with the help of a demon from some other dimension, of course – but they'd assumed he could, at the very least, use that magic to find them.

He doesn't have to find Wally, she thought with more than a trace of bitterness. *But he could still find me.*

She hesitated a moment longer. She could simply zip across the water and see Aunt Phyllis in person, of course…but she didn't want to do that. She didn't want Aunt Phyllis to know where she was, for her own safety, and she particularly didn't want Aunt Phyllis to know that she'd been hiding out just a couple of hundred metres away without bothering to make her presence known. And she couldn't be *entirely* certain Major didn't have a second watcher posted somewhere nearby.

She lifted the handset, heard the dial tone, and dialed.

One ring…two rings…she wondered, if she stuck her head out the front door, if she'd be able to hear it ringing across the water.

The ringing stopped. "Hello?" said Aunt Phyllis's voice.

Ariane suddenly found her throat had gone dry. She couldn't speak.

"Hello?" Aunt Phyllis said again, sounding a little irritated.

"Hi," Ariane managed to croak at last. "Hi, Aunt Phyllis."

"Ariane?" Even over the old phone line, Ariane could hear the immense relief in Aunt Phyllis's voice. "Where are you? Are you still in France?"

"No," Ariane said. "I'm back."

"Back? Back where? Canada?" Now Aunt Phyllis's voice changed. "Then why aren't you here?"

"I..." Ariane swallowed. "Aunt Phyllis, I...I don't dare join you."

"What? Don't be ridiculous, Ariane, you have to."

"I can't, Aunt Phyllis," Ariane said miserably. "It's not safe. If Rex Major finds out I made it back safely, he might kidnap you to try to make me give up my shard of Excalibur."

"*Your* shard...you mean he has the other one?" Aunt Phyllis said. "How did that happen?"

"Wally," Ariane said. "It was Wally."

"Wally?" Aunt Phyllis said. "I don't understand..."

"He betrayed me," Ariane said. Those words, too, were hard to force out of her throat. "He lied to me. He joined Merlin. He tricked me into giving him one of the shards. And then he left me all alone." Even now the horror of that moment when she had come out of the shower to discover Wally and the second shard gone brought tears to her eyes...tears, and anger.

Anger that flowed from the shard as much as from her. Once again she felt the flood of ice-cold rage the sword was so good at generating. *Kill your enemies, make them pay, take revenge...*

I'll make him pay, she assured it. *I will.*

"Wally?" Aunt Phyllis said. "I can't believe it. Ariane, he must just be tricking Rex Major. I'll bet he's got some scheme to get the shard for you."

"I *had* the shard," Ariane said harshly. "I had it, and he stole it. Wally Knight is my enemy, Aunt Phyllis. As much as Rex Major."

"Ariane..."

"I just called to tell you I'm all right," she said. "And that I can't join you. And that you're being watched. I'm going after the third shard. Just stay put and you should be fine."

"Ariane, no," Aunt Phyllis said. "You can't do this alone. You need my help. Come to Emma Lake. There must be some way you can get into the cabin without being seen. We can talk, figure things out –"

"No, Aunt Phyllis," Ariane said. "This is my quest. Mine alone. I'll let you know when I have the third shard."

"Ariane –"

Ariane hung up. She stared at the phone in the cradle. *That was a mistake*, she thought. *I shouldn't even have called her. Now she's going to worry even more.*

Then she thought, *I can't stay here.*

That much she was certain of. Not only was she out of food and water, but Major's man would be back in a couple of hours, settling into the cabin to keep a leisurely watch on Aunt Phyllis, waiting for Ariane to make an appearance.

He can rot here, Ariane thought viciously. *I won't be anywhere near.*

But then…where?

She couldn't go back to the house she'd shared with Aunt Phyllis in Regina. She was sure Major must be watching it, too. But she had to have *somewhere* to stay. She needed fresh clothes. She needed food. And she needed somewhere with water, a pool deep enough to cover her, deep enough for her to materialize in…

And then it hit her. The perfect solution, and she couldn't believe she hadn't thought of it before.

Wally's house.

It had a swimming pool. It was empty: Wally's parents had separated; Wally was with Rex Major; and his sister, Felicia – Flish – was still in hospital, and had moved out weeks ago, so she wouldn't be returning to the house even after she was released. Last time Ariane had been there, the cupboards and fridge had been stuffed with food. Mrs. Carson had been hired to look after the Knight siblings, but with both of them gone, she wouldn't be living there – although she might still be checking on the house once a day. But all Ariane needed to do to dodge Mrs. Carson, or anyone else who might come into the place, was to run water in the sink.

As long as she was careful, she could live in Wally's house undetected, for as long as she needed...until the third shard manifested itself. And the fact she'd be living rent-free at Wally's expense just made it all that much more perfect.

She glanced around the old cabin. Everything looked the same as she had left it when she'd gotten up that morning. She didn't disturb it – she didn't want Major's man noticing anything had changed. No doubt he was wondering if she'd been there, but he couldn't be sure it had been anything more than a tramp. And that meant Rex Major couldn't be sure.

She was still one step ahead. For the moment.

She slipped out the back door, went down to the lakeshore, and let the water take her away.

CHAPTER TWO

THE LAP OF LUXURY

"I'M A TWEET WITTLE BIRDIE 'N A GILDED CAGE, *Tweety's my name but I don't know my age. I don't have to wowwy and dat is dat, I'm safe in here from dat old putty tat!*" sang Tweety Bird.

Tweety Bird, Wally Knight reflected, looked downright alarming when viewed on a wall-sized television, especially with Mel Blanc's voice likewise amplified by speakers that wouldn't have looked out of place at a rock concert.

All the same, he knew how Tweety felt. At least the "wittle birdie 'n a gilded cage" part, if not the "safe in here from dat old putty tat" part. Because even though he'd only been in Rex Major's penthouse condominium for four days, and even though it was by far and away the most luxurious place he'd ever been, it was also, very clearly, a cage.

He'd said as much to Major that morning, as his host was preparing to go out. "I've been stuck in here since we got back," he'd complained. "I just want to go downstairs, walk around the block."

"No," Major said. "You're only fourteen –"

"Fifteen in a couple of months," Wally interjected.

"Fourteen," Major repeated firmly, "and you're in a strange city. I don't want you wandering around by yourself."

"My Mom grew up in Toronto and was taking the subway by herself all over town when she was twelve," Wally argued. "I got to Lyon, France, on my own. I don't think I'm likely to get abducted from the lakefront!"

"The lakefront?" Major said. "Think about that. We don't know what Ariane will do." He pointed at Wally's face. "You just got the stitches out yesterday from what she did to you in France."

Wally rubbed his cheek. The cut where the second shard of Excalibur had sliced his cheek as Ariane called it to herself was still healing, and was at the angry-red-scar stage. He'd been told to rub it with petroleum jelly every day and that it should eventually all-but-disappear. Which he'd also been told about the wound on his forehead from slipping and falling on the ice and knocking himself out just a few days before the sword-shard-in-the-face incident. Unfortunately, neither wound had left a mark he could pass off as either the result of having survived an attack by Voldemort as a baby or fighting a duel with rapiers in Heidelberg. They just made him look like he must be incredibly clumsy.

"You're too valuable to me," Major said. "I can't risk anything happening to you."

"You keep saying I'm something special," Wally complained, "but you never tell me *why*."

"Because I'm still not certain, Wally," Major said. "Give me time. Now I have to go. Stay put and we'll talk more tonight." And then he'd gone, locking the door behind him.

Which might not have been enough to keep Wally in, except he'd also stationed a "bodyguard" in the short hallway outside which led to the elevator. Wally wondered how he'd explained the man's presence to the condo board. Then he snorted. *He's Rex Major. I doubt he has to explain much of anything.*

After four days in the condo, amazing though it was – six bedrooms, a dining room bigger than the main floor of Ariane's whole house, a kitchen grand enough to host a *Top Chef* episode (maybe it had, for all he knew) and even a swimming pool (empty: Major wasn't taking any chances), he was going stir crazy.

He had television. But he didn't have the Internet. There was a library, but the books seemed to have been chosen more for bragging rights than content, as Wally discovered when he pulled down an enticing leather-bound volume only to find out it was an eighteenth-century Spanish/Latin dictionary with the catchy title of *Dictionarium emendatum, auctum, locuplectatum*, edited by one Elio Antonio de Nebrija. Very impressive, no doubt, probably valuable, and useful should he suffer from insomnia, but otherwise...

All the other books seemed to be in the same vein. He couldn't find a single one that was even in English.

Which was how he had ended up sprawled on the couch in the media room yet again, watching old Warner Brothers cartoons blown up to terrifying size.

But today was going to be different, because today he had a plan. He was just waiting long enough to make sure Major was really gone and wasn't going to pop back in unexpectedly for something he'd forgotten, and to establish in the mind of the guard (who presumably could hear at least something of Sylvester's "Suffering succotash!" through the door), that he was watching TV.

And he'd probably waited long enough.

He got up and went into the living room, a vast expanse of marble floor with a minimum of furniture and a maximum of window, overlooking Lake Ontario – well, overlooking its own enormous terrace, actually, and *then* overlooking Lake Ontario – and padded in his stocking feet across to the door on the far side.

It was the only door that was always closed. It was the only door that was always locked. It had a combination keypad to ensure it stayed that way. And Wally had watched from the far side of the room as Rex Major had put in the combination just that morning, peering around the corner of the hallway that led to his own bedroom, then drawing back and emerging yawning and stretching a few minutes later.

He'd decided back in France that Merlin was more to be trusted than the Lady of the Lake, and that in order to save Ariane from herself, and from the pernicious influence of the shards of Excalibur, he had to help Major get the remaining shards. But trusting Major more than the Lady of the Lake wasn't the same thing as trusting Major completely. Wally didn't trust the Lady of the Lake at all. Trusting Major a little bit more than that was still a pretty small measure of trust.

And Major was keeping something from him. He kept talking about how Wally might be someone special, as special in his own way as Ariane. But he wouldn't tell Wally what he meant until he could be certain. And for some reason, even after four days and even though he had the second shard in his possession, he still couldn't be certain. Or at least he *pretended* he couldn't be certain.

Wally was tired of waiting. And he was tired of being locked up, no matter how gilded the cage. He'd thought by now he'd at least have a tutor coming in, and much to his surprise, he wished he did: better homework than another *Buffy the Vampire Slayer* marathon, much though he liked the old show. But, no.

Well, then, he'd make his own homework and entertainment.

He keyed in the code he'd seen Major use and, without any fuss, the door unlocked. He opened it.

As he'd expected, the room beyond was Major's home office, though it looked more like a set piece in an office supply store than a real office. Not a sheet of paper on the desk. No photos of family members, no Newton's Cradle desk toy with the little swinging silver balls, nothing but an impressively large monitor, a wireless keyboard and mouse, a surprisingly minimalist desk chair, light grey walls, dark grey carpet, and a little bar complete with sink, refrigerator, an assortment of bottles, and a glass-fronted cabinet full of glasses. And, of course, a massive window with a view of Lake Ontario, just like the rest of the condo.

Wally sat down at the desk and jiggled the mouse. The screen lit up and asked for a password.

Wally had a theory: that Rex Major, despite heading up a fabulously successful high-tech company, was old-fashioned, as befitted someone who had once been Merlin, court wizard and power behind the throne of King Arthur, and probably wasn't really all that comfortable with modern technology. That theory had generated a hypothesis: that Merlin's password was unlikely to be very complex or hard for him to remember.

And now, to complete the scientific process, Wally was going to put his hypothesis to the experimental test. It might take a while, but, *Hey*, he thought, *I've got all day.*

First, the obvious. *PASSWORD*, he typed.

No luck.

MERLIN was next.

That didn't work either.

EXCALIBUR failed. So did *FAERIE, ARTHUR,* and *KINGARTHUR.*

He thought for a moment. Major's real concern, or so he'd always claimed, wasn't Earth at all. Seizing control of Earth through the magical power he would have once

Excalibur was his was only the first step. He wanted to use Earth's advanced technology to attack and conquer his own world: the realm of Faerie.

FAERIE had failed as a password. But Merlin's first target would be his family's demesne, he'd said: a name with a long history in Arthurian legend, for reasons Wally now understood.

Worth a shot, he thought.

He typed *AVALON*.

And just like that, he had access to Rex Major's computer.

All Merlin would have had to do was add three or four numbers or letters after that and I'd have never figured it out, Wally thought. *Hypothesis confirmed, theory looking good.*

He cracked his knuckles and set to work to find out everything he could that Merlin didn't want him to know.

◄◄ ►►

In his office high atop the Excalibur Computer Systems tower, Merlin stared at a different computer screen without really seeing the financial spreadsheet on it. His mind was on an entirely different problem than maximizing the quarterly profits. He was trying to figure out how to find the third shard of Excalibur.

He had thought, with one shard of the sword in hand, he would be able to sense the location of the third piece even though Ariane Forsythe still had the first. He had no idea where she was: there'd been no trace of her since they'd parted ways in France. He supposed it was possible she had died in the attempt to return across the Atlantic, but he thought it unlikely, since if she were dead, whatever interference her having the first shard was causing, in his use of the second should have vanished – and that interference was definitely still there. To his ongoing frustration, he could not draw on the power of the shard he held to bolster the pitiful sliver of magic left to him since the Lady had fled the world and tried to close the door to Faerie behind her.

He fingered the ruby stud he always wore in his right earlobe. That door remained open, just a crack, so he was not *completely* without magic, but it galled him every day how puny he was compared to the old days in Arthur's court, when he had commanded powers that had caused whole armies to throw down their arms and surrender.

Most of the power remaining to him he had infused into his Excalibur software, piggy-backing on the World Wide Web to cast a barely-there skein of magic around the globe. It was through that magic – ironically present in Wally Knight's own smartphone – that he had detected the Lady's presence when she had materialized in Wascana Lake in Regina and convinced Ariane to assume her mantle of power and seek the shards of Excalibur. The same magic had found the first shard for him in a diamond mine in Yellowknife, though he had lost that one to Ariane in the end. His magic had found the second shard for him, in an ancient cave complex in the south of France. But so far, it had not found the third, and he couldn't even bolster it with power from the second.

The third shard could reveal itself at any moment, of course. All it would take was someone with a smartphone or laptop or other Internet-connected device to get close enough to it. But even the World Wide Web had enormous holes in it where something as small as a piece of a sword blade could hide forever.

His one consolation was that Ariane should be experiencing the same frustration. She could not draw on the power of the shard she carried, either, and that meant that if the third shard were as distant from her as the second had been, she didn't yet know where it was.

In Yellowknife, he had convinced her to hand over the first shard – though she had later stolen it back again – by threatening her friend, Wally Knight. That was unlikely to work this time, since Wally had betrayed her in France – a coup which gave Major no small satisfaction. But he had another possible lever. Even now, he had two men from Ochrana Security, the private firm he used when he didn't want Excalibur Computer Systems directly involved, watching the cabin at Emma Lake where Aunt Phyllis had gone to ground. He had hoped every day to hear that Ariane had made an appearance there, and had laid plans for that eventuality, but so far there'd been no sign of...

Right on cue, a small box popped up on his screen announcing the arrival of an email message from one of the Ochrana Security man at Emma Lake. *Magic!* Major thought, then snorted. *Never attribute to supernatural causes what can be ascribed to coincidence.* Although to be fair, he'd made good use of coincidence in the past to bolster other people's belief in his omnipotence. A certain eclipse came to mind...

Even as he was thinking that, he was opening the email. He read it over, and smiled slowly. *Rented cabin across from subject's for easier surveillance,* his prime watcher had written. *No sign of the girl at her aunt's, but the rental cabin had been broken into and someone had been camping there for at least a day or two. Could be coincidence.*

Could be, Major thought. But just because coincidence could account for many "supernatural" experiences didn't mean it was the best explanation for *everything.* And this coincidence seemed unlikely in the extreme.

She's alive. I don't know where she is, but that doesn't really matter. Because now that I know she's alive, I can pull the other lever I have for getting her to cooperate.

He clicked *Reply* and typed, *Be prepared to apprehend the subject on my order,* as previously discussed.

He clicked *Send.*

He stared at the spreadsheet again, but still didn't see it. *The boy could be a problem if he finds out,* he thought. *He's got a soft spot for Phyllis Forsythe.* He snorted. *And for Ariane. Fortunately enough. He thinks betraying her was for her own good.*

Although to be fair to him, in a way, it was. *If she'd give up on the search for Excalibur I won't be forced to keep threatening her and the people she loves. You'd think she'd see that.*

He sighed. She was being blinded by his sister's influence, of course. Once she'd assumed the Lady's power, she'd also assumed something of the Lady's attitudes. He didn't believe for a moment that Ariane would give up trying to defeat him, no matter what he did. But he *did* think she was still enough of an ordinary fifteen-year-old that he could confuse her and frighten her – and thus get her to act against the Lady's programming. Just as he had confused Wally enough to get him to act against what Ariane wanted.

Merlin had always been very good at sowing confusion. However much his magical power might have waned, that power still remained to him, even without using his magical Voice of Command, which didn't work against Wally – his first hint the boy might be Arthur's heir – or Ariane, because she held the power of his sister.

Still, if Wally found out about Phyllis…

I need to distract him, Merlin thought. *I need him thinking more about himself and less about Ariane and the sword. I need to dangle something shiny in front of him.*

And I have just the thing.

He picked up the phone and dialed his own home number.

Most of the files on Rex Major's home computer proved disappointing to Wally: endless, detailed reports about every aspect of Excalibur Computer Systems. If he'd been interested in industrial espionage, Wally could have been a hero to hackers everywhere within the first five minutes – but that wasn't what he was after.

He wanted to know, first and foremost, what Major knew about *him*.

A simple search for his name turned up a whole file, buried in nested folders about ten layers deep. He opened it, and blinked at just how much information it contained. All his school records. The IQ test he'd taken once and had never seen the results of. He opened that first. "Near-genius," he muttered. "What do you mean, *near*?" He closed the file, opened another.

There were photos of him going to and from school, photos of his house, photos of him with Ariane, video of him at a swimming lesson in the YMCA, shot from the glassed-in parents' waiting area at one end of the pool. He watched his skinny body flail its way from one end of the pool to the other with way too much splashing, and sighed. A natural athlete, he wasn't.

It was all very creepy and invasive and pretty much exactly what he'd expected. But there was nothing there that even hinted at the deep, dark secret Major was harbouring about whatever mysterious power Wally was supposed to have.

Maybe I should tell him what Ariane told me happened when I held both shards and placed them together – how they sang in perfect harmony instead of disharmony in her mind…

No, he decided. *Not yet. I'm not ready to share* all *my secrets with him.*

He looked at the still-playing video of his swimming lesson, and snorted. *Not that I haven't already shared way too much without knowing it. Am I* really *that scrawny?*

He closed all the files, closed the folder, and opened one labelled A. Forsythe. It was much the same as his, only even creepier: one video clip had been shot with a telephoto lens through her bedroom window, and showed her sitting in her pajamas, brushing her hair. He looked at the other video files of her and decided not to open them in case they showed something even more private, and felt a flash of anger at Rex Major. However much his arguments against the Lady and in favour of his gaining possession of Excalibur held water, the man was manipulative and ruthless, and Wally had better not forget it.

There was another file folder labelled "P. Forsythe," presumably full of similar surveillance material on Phyllis.

And then he blinked.

There was a third file folder labelled Forsythe, but the first initial was E.

E. Forsythe.

Emily Forsythe.

Ariane's mother!

Wally moved the cursor over to the file…

…and the phone rang.

He jerked, startled. The cursor flew across the screen. He reached out and picked up the handset. "Hell…hello?"

"Wally," said Rex Major. "I've decided you're right."

"I…am?"

"I've decided you deserve to get out of the condo. I'm texting the man out front while we speak. He'll come in and bring you downtown. There's something I'd like your help with…"

"Um…great," Wally said, even as he frantically closed everything he had opened, turned off the monitor – no, wait, it had been on, but asleep – turned it back on, pushed back the chair, shoved it in just the way it had been as best as he could remember, and darted for the door, handset still in hand.

Rex Major kept talking, oblivious – at least, Wally *hoped* he was oblivious – to Wally's desperate rush for safety. "It's a big secret – don't tell anyone! – but we've established a game division and we've got a couple of projects we're just about to release for beta testing. I'd love to have you be the first beta tester, in-house, give the team some pointers from the point of view of the target audience."

"What...what kind of game?" Wally gasped, hoping he didn't sound as breathless as he felt as he closed the office door behind him and dashed for the long white couch facing the expansive window.

He'd just flopped himself onto it when the front door of the condo opened and the burly black bodyguard stepped in.

Major laughed. "It's a sword-and-sorcery, first-person adventure game set in the court of King Arthur, of course."

Wally laughed a little weakly. "Ha-ha. Of course."

The bodyguard was looking at him through narrowed eyes. "I'm to take you down to Mr. Major's office," he growled. "You ready?"

"Just need my shoes," Wally said brightly, and then to Major, "We're on our way."

"See you shortly," Major said.

He hung up. The bodyguard stood inside the front door, arms folded.

"You can wait outside," Wally said to him. "I'll just be a minute."

The bodyguard didn't move. "I'll wait here."

"Suit yourself!" Wally said with a grin, and carefully

put the handset down on the glass-and-chrome coffee table.

The handset he had brought out of Major's locked office.

Feeling as if he'd left a time bomb sitting out in full view, he went in search of his shoes.

CHAPTER THREE

BEHIND ENEMY LINES

ARIANE DIDN'T GO STRAIGHT to the Knight house in Regina. She thought it might be safer to wait until night. Instead she transported herself to Saskatoon, climbing out of the South Saskatchewan River at a spot where the brush along its southern shore provided some cover. A short hike and a steep climb later she was on Broadway Avenue. She had no money, but as she stood outside Starbucks, looking in longingly, a woman in a smart red business suit and black fur-lined jacket came out, took in her hungry expression and tattered and dirty clothes, and pressed five dollars into her hands. "Good luck," she said, and then hurried away while Ariane gaped after her, too shocked to say anything.

She thinks I'm a...homeless person, she thought, feeling outraged.

And then the cold truth hit her: in a very real sense, she *was*.

She took her five dollars and went into Starbucks for coffee and something sweet to eat.

She kicked around downtown Saskatoon for the rest of the day. Late in the afternoon, as twilight gathered and the downtown workers headed for home, she made her way down to the river again, stomach again growling with hunger, and almost eagerly flung herself into the cold water.

She surfaced in the Knight swimming pool in the house on Harrington Mews, and for a frightening instant thought she wasn't alone. The only lights in the window-less room came from the pale blue glimmering lamps just beneath the surface, and it was in that dim glow she saw what she thought was a person standing at the pool's edge. She almost let herself dissolve back into the water before she realized all she was seeing was the little diving plat-form at the deep end, covered with a tarp.

Gulping, she swam to the edge, clambered out, and or-dered herself dry. Then she stood a moment to let her eyes adjust before creeping over to the door leading from the pool enclosure into the main part of the house. She pressed her ear against it and listened.

Nothing.

She opened it.

The hallway beyond stretched a short distance to the living room, past the downstairs half-bath on the left and the door to the basement stairs on the right, underneath the stairs up to the main floor. The journey from Saska-toon had taken long enough that full night had fallen out-side and all was in shadow, the only light the slight illumination that seeped in through curtained windows from street lamps outside. Ariane crept down the hall and, a moment later, was peering into the painfully neat main room of the Knight house. It had a palpably un-lived-in feel, but that didn't mean there was no one asleep upstairs. She *thought* Flish was still in the hospital, and wasn't living here anyway, and she *didn't* think Mrs. Car-son would be staying there with neither of the children to look after, but she wasn't a hundred percent sure. So, just to be safe, she cautiously crept up the stairs and listened at each of the four doors in turn before opening them and peering in.

The first room was Wally's. She'd never been in it, but she doubted anyone else in his family would make their main decorating motif superhero movie posters seasoned with a dash of *Star Wars* and a soupçon of *The Hobbit*.

The next room she knew was...or had been...Felicia's. She'd spent an enjoyable few minutes one day trashing it. She eased open the door. The room looked just the way she remembered it, except it had been stripped of everything personal. It was no one's room now.

At the end of the hall she found the master bedroom. It had its own bathroom, complete with Jacuzzi, but it felt as painfully empty as Flish's. Wally's parents had separated, and even when his Dad had flown in right after their adventures in Yellowknife, he hadn't stayed in the house. And he'd flown out again the next day after dropping the separation news on Wally. Wally's Mom had been out of town for weeks, working on a series of movies. Apparently she was beginning to make a name for herself as an assistant producer. Ariane had never heard of any of the movies she'd worked on.

Ariane hadn't met either of Wally's parents. She didn't think she wanted to.

The fourth room, on the same side of the hall as the bathroom where Ariane had first discovered her ability to command water off her body, after she and Wally had had their first damp encounter with the Lady of the Lake, had to be the guest room...and Mrs. Carson's when she was there.

She listened. She heard nothing.

She eased the door open a crack, listened harder.

Still nothing.

She pushed it open all the way.

The room was as empty as all the rest: emptier, because the bed had been stripped, the mattress left bare and slightly askew, and the drawers of the chest of drawers were half open. *Looks like Mrs. Carson left in a snit*, Ariane thought. *Won't hurt Wally's feelings.*

And then she remembered anew what Wally had done, and felt a flash of anger, aimed at herself, for even *thinking* of Wally's feelings.

Certain at last that she was alone in the house, she went back to Felicia's room. She knew Flish had moved out, but she thought there was at least a chance the older girl had left behind some of her clothes, especially stuff she'd outgrown…stuff that might fit Ariane.

She was in luck. The jeans were tighter than she usually wore and the only top she could find was shorter than she would have liked, flashing her midriff at every move, but it was better than her own filthy and worse-for-wear garb, which, once she'd changed, she promptly took downstairs and threw into the Knights' washing machine.

Then she explored the kitchen. The light from the refrigerator seemed dangerously bright when she swung the door open, and she hastily swung it mostly closed again. She found bread and cheese and sandwich meat. There was also half a cold pizza but she had no idea how old it was. A few cans of Coke rested on the bottom shelf. She cracked one open and drank it while she made herself a sandwich, which she ate sitting on the stools by the granite-topped island.

With food in her belly, she suddenly felt terribly tired. She moved her clothes from the washer to the dryer, then trudged back up the stairs.

She'd thought she'd sleep in Felicia's room, but as she passed Wally's a new surge of anger at his betrayal drove away her fatigue, and with a feeling of perverse pleasure she went into his room instead.

His bed boasted a Spiderman bedspread that had probably been there since he was eight. There was a Spongebob Squarepants nightlight. There were the posters she'd seen before, and there were books – lots and lots of books, from *Percy Jackson* to *The Hunger Games* to *The Maze Runner* to others she'd never heard of. His closet had very few clothes in it – just a few pairs of jeans. His chest of drawers contained underwear – some of the older pairs of which also featured superheroes, Superman and Batman and the Flash – and socks, along with a remarkably varied array of T-shirts with geeky slogans or pictures on them. Drawers under his bed contained toys from when he was a little boy. A desk facing the window held a computer monitor, keyboard, and mouse. The computer itself peeked out from underneath.

Ariane stared around the room and felt tears start in her eyes. But the self-pity was soon washed away by another flood of rage. Wally had been her friend. He'd been her companion in the quest the Lady had given them. She'd trusted him, more than she'd ever trusted anyone else in her whole life. And he'd betrayed her. He'd betrayed her to the man who had threatened her, who had threatened *him*. He'd lied to her. He'd stolen the second shard of Excalibur, the sword forged by the Lady of the Lake, her ancestor.

The sword is mine, she thought. *Mine. And he stole part of it!*

And with that thought, the anger blazed in her so hot she felt on fire. She stepped onto Wally's bed. She ripped down the *Star Wars* poster over his bed, the *Iron Man* poster next to it, the *Avengers* poster, the *Hobbit* poster, *all* the posters. She ripped them down and ripped them up and cast the torn pieces around the room. Then she pulled out the drawers and upended them, dragged the clothes from the closet and tossed them to the floor, pulled the toys from under his bed and threw them as hard as she could against the walls, smashing some of them into broken bits of plastic that bounced all over the room.

And when all that was done, she threw herself on his bed, fists clenched, eyes scrunched shut.

The pillow smelled like Wally.

She burst into tears.

She cried for a long time, then dozed for a while. Finally, feeling drained but with the weight of her earlier fatigue gone, she sat up again.

I really made a mess of his room, she thought, looking around, but despite all the annoying waterworks she'd just had to work her way through, she couldn't feel very sorry about it. Excalibur's point, strapped to her side, seemed to surge with cold fire. *No, not sorry at all.*

But even though she could feel the sword there, even though she could feel the power within it, she knew she couldn't call on it. And that frustrated her. She'd still heard nothing from the third shard of Excalibur. It could be literally anywhere on the planet – well, anywhere the Lady had been able to reach by way of clouds and fresh water, which didn't exactly narrow down the possible locations enough to be useful.

But then she blinked as a thought hit her. She might not be able to find the shard – but she might be able to figure out where Rex Major was, so that if he had found the shard, she might be able to race him to it as she had in France.

She swung her feet over the edge of the bed and, walking across one torn half of Wally's *The Desolation of Smaug* poster, went to his desk. She shoved underwear and socks off his swivel chair and sat down. He had a widescreen monitor: she found the button and turned it on, then turned on the computer tower under the desk.

Even if he had a password set she could probably log in as a guest user...

But he didn't have a password set. The computer booted up normally. *Careless, Wally*, she thought. She opened the browser, then hesitated. Merlin could be monitoring Wally's computer, she knew. *But why would he?* she reasoned. *He* knows *where Wally is.*

Deciding it was worth the risk, she typed "Rex Major" into Google, set the search terms for the past week, and clicked the magnifying glass button to begin the search.

◄◄ ►►

Throughout the drive to Excalibur Computer Systems, Wally thought about the handset on the coffee table. The guard hadn't seemed to notice it, but the second Rex Major saw it he'd know that Wally had been in his office. And then...

What?

Wally didn't know. Major seemed to need him. And he still thought Major had the right idea about what needed to be done with Excalibur. But that didn't mean he thought Major wasn't capable of doing really nasty things, possibly even to him.

Definitely to Ariane.

And that brought him back to the file folder he had spotted just before he'd had to call a sudden halt to his *Spy Kids* exploits. E. Forsythe. Emily Forsythe. Could Major have had something to do with Ariane's mother's disappearance?

Or even more intriguing...was it possible he knew where she was?

Not for the first time, Wally felt the urgent need to talk to Ariane. But he couldn't. He had burned that line of communication pretty thoroughly by stealing the second shard of Excalibur from her, even if he had left her the first to help her get home. He was trying to protect her, trying to keep her safe, but he didn't suppose she'd quite worked her way around to believing that yet. And with her power, and the influence Excalibur was exerting on her mind and emotions – well, Major was probably right that Wally was better off well out of her reach.

Even if that did mean the penthouse swimming pool had had to be drained.

Still, even if she wanted to kill him, she might still listen to him, if only he could get a message to her. The trouble was, he didn't know where she was. And he didn't have the faintest idea how to find out.

He didn't even know if she was all right.

He pushed that thought aside. Of *course* she was all right. She'd flown across the Atlantic to France on her own, jumping in incorporeal form from cloud to cloud. She could certainly have returned the same way. He'd made sure she still had one shard of Excalibur for that very reason.

No, she was fine. She had to be. She was just hiding from Major.

Which meant she was hiding from him, too. Which meant the only chance Wally was likely to have to give her any message at all was if Major found her.

He massaged his temples with his right hand. Being the loyal sidekick in a fantasy adventure had been a piece of cake compared to being the misunderstood character whose conscience had forced him to commit apparent treason in order to protect the heroine while at the same time helping the tragic villain who really wasn't a villain at all, just misunderstood.

Or something like that.

Wally Knight, he admonished himself, *you read too much.*

The car pulled up in front of a towering building of black glass and dark red stone, and turned right down a ramp into a massive underground parking garage. His taciturn driver pulled straight into an extra-wide spot right by the elevators: *REX MAJOR*, read the metal sign on the concrete wall, in gold letters on a burnished black background. The driver got out. He came around to open Wally's door for him, but Wally was already out by the time he got there. "Thanks, big guy," Wally said. "What's your name, anyway?"

The guard didn't answer. He just pointed at the elevators. He didn't push a button to call one: instead he swiped a keycard.

Together they rode up...and up...and up...sixty floors by the time they were done, and nobody else got on the elevator all the way up. *Private parking and override control of elevators so he doesn't have to share*, Wally thought. *Now, that's power.*

The elevator didn't take them into a general lobby area, either, but what was obviously a private hallway, with only two doors: one marked *EXIT* to their right, and one marked with a discreet Excalibur Computer Systems logo to their left. The guard used his keycard again to unlock that door and they stepped through.

Rex Major sat at a large and uncluttered desk in a surprisingly modern office. They had entered behind him, through a door that disappeared completely into the grey padded panelling when the guard closed it. To Wally's left, a wall of glass offered a spectacular view of the Toronto skyline and Lake Ontario beyond. He could see Major's condo building. It looked small from the top of *this* tower.

To his right was a black conference table with six white chairs pulled up to it, plus a counter with a sink and cabinets of some black wood above and below. Opposite

Major's black desk were two white leather chairs. A considerable distance beyond them, forcing anyone who came into the room the normal way to walk a long distance to reach the man at the desk, was the main entrance into the office, double doors of that same shining black wood. The artwork ran to the blocky-fields-of-primary-colours abstract, and the lighting was mostly hidden in sconces pointing upward around the office's edges, except for the extraordinarily ostentatious chandelier of about a dozen concentric rings of dangling crystal rods in the exact centre of the room.

Major was studying an Excel spreadsheet. He glanced their way as they entered, and then swung his chair toward them. "Excellent," he said. "You can go, Emeka."

The big black man nodded once, then turned and went out the way he had come.

Major got up and went over to the bar. "Something to drink?" he asked Wally.

"Vodka martini. Shaken, not stirred."

He didn't really expect Major to get the reference. James Bond was a pretty recent invention to a millennium-old wizard. But Major surprised him. "I may be an evil mastermind but I'm not Dr. No," he said dryly. "And you're no double-oh seven. How about a Diet Coke?"

Wally sighed. "Works for me."

Major pulled a bottle of Diet Coke out of a refrigerator hidden in the lower cabinets for Wally, and retrieved a bottle of Perrier for himself. He gestured at the conference table. Wally sat and opened the bottle. Major sat opposite him and opened his. They drank together.

"Any word on Ariane?" Wally asked as he lowered his bottle.

Major shook his head. "None. I hope she's all right."

I hope you mean that, Wally thought. "Any sense of where the third shard is?"

"Not yet," Major said. "But I hope to know something soon."

"I don't suppose you're ready to tell me what it is you suspect about *me*," Wally said.

Major shook his head again. "No," he said. "I can't confirm it until I have two of the shards. It's too bad you were only able to get one of them away from Ariane. Otherwise I'd not only be able to confirm what I think might be true about you, I'd be able to go straight to the third shard."

And Ariane might have died trying to make it across the Atlantic, Wally thought. *Maybe she did anyway.*

No, he told himself again. *She's not dead. She can't be. I'd know.*

Wouldn't I?

No you wouldn't, he forced himself to admit. *You don't believe in telepathy.*

Of course, he hadn't believed in magic until recently, either.

He took another swig of Diet Coke. "So…this game you were telling me about. You really want my help beta-testing it?"

"I really do," Major said. "Although it's more like alpha-testing. Right now nobody outside the company even knows we're developing it."

"You hope," Wally said.

"I *know*," Major said. "Excalibur Computer Systems has…very high standards of corporate loyalty." He smiled.

Command, Wally thought. *He could simply Command everyone working on the game to keep quiet about it.*

But he can't Command me. Why?

"Well…tell me about the game," Wally said.

"I'd rather show you," Major said. He stood up. "Let me take you to our skunkworks."

An hour later Wally, wearing a skin-tight suit wired

with sensors and a pair of virtual-reality goggles, stood in the middle of a room he couldn't see – because his eyes were showing him, in splendid 3D high-definition, the great hall of a castle.

The room was hung with shields and crossed spears and ancient banners, some moth-eaten, some that looked brand-new, some stained with blood. A fire burned in a pit in the middle of the hall, the smoke rising up to a hole in the peaked wooden roof far above. The flames crackled and popped in his headphones just like the real thing. All that was missing was the smell, and the heat.

In his gloved right hand Wally held a plastic rod weighted to feel like a broadsword. In the game, it *was* a broadsword, catching the light of the fire as he swung it experimentally through the air.

Across the fire, at the far end of the hall, stood two giant wooden doors, bound with iron, each twice as tall as he was. As he watched, they swung inward, and into the hall strode a knight, wearing a black surcoat over black mail, helmet closed, sword in hand. "King Arthur!" boomed the knight. "I challenge you to a duel to the death!"

Wally felt his cheeks stretch as he grinned. He couldn't help it.

This, he thought, *is the coolest game ever.*

He hefted the sword. "Challenge accepted!" he shouted, and dashed forward.

◄◄ ►►

Rex Major watched as the boy sparred with the virtual knight. "Wow," said Howard Gustin, the lead programmer, who was watching with him. "That kid knows what he's doing. We had top swordmasters in here when we were programming the Black Knight, and he's more than holding his own. He's a natural."

You have no idea, Major thought.

He turned to go. "Wally's yours for the rest of the day," he said. "Emeka will pick him up at quitting time. I have to fly out this afternoon."

"Where are you off to, sir?" Gustin said.

"Can't tell you, Howie," Major said. He smiled. "Well, I could, but then I'd have to kill you."

Gustin laughed.

Major let the smile slip away as he turned to go out. He didn't really care if Howard Gustin knew where he was going, but he didn't want *Wally* to know. He'd already made the arrangements for his private jet to take him to Prince Albert. He'd spend the night there.

And early tomorrow...he was looking forward to meeting Aunt Phyllis.

He smiled again.

Yes, he was looking forward to meeting her very much.

CHAPTER FOUR

MAJOR MAKES A MOVE

WALLY SPENT A VERY PLEASANT DAY in the "skunkworks."
At lunchtime, while he enjoyed a hamburger and fries in the
company dining room, Howard Gustin, the lead designer,
pumped him for information about how he had interacted
with the game, what he thought of the virtual-reality
headset, his opinion of the graphics...even asked for his
input on the title. "We're thinking of calling it *Sword Art
Online*," Gustin said.

Wally laughed. "I think that's taken."

The designer raised an eyebrow. "Really?"

"Anime series about a bunch of gamers getting trapped
in an online virtual-reality game," he explained. "A lot of
them die. Probably not the vibe you're going for."

Gustin laughed ruefully. "Probably not." He put a line
through one of a long list of titles on a sheet of paper on
the clipboard he carried. "How about..."

At the end of a few more hours in the virtual-reality
suit clobbering bad guys, Wally emerged from the
skunkworks feeling rather like a skunk himself. He was
already worrying about the telephone handset he'd left in
plain sight in Major's living room: with a clue that big,

Major could hardly fail to figure out Wally had been somewhere he wasn't supposed to be. But Major wasn't waiting for him in the hallway: Emeka was.

"I'm here to take you home," Emeka said.

"Where's Rex?" Wally said. He was pretty sure Emeka would never refer to Rex Major by his first name.

He was right. "*Mister* Major," Emeka said, "has had to fly out of town on business."

"That's too bad," Wally said, while inwardly heaving a sigh of relief. And then... "So I'll have the place to myself?"

"You will be guarded as usual, but yes, you will be alone in the suite," Emeka said. "Supper is being delivered."

"Movie night," Wally said out loud, but what he was thinking was, *A whole night to dig through Major's computer.* "Can't wait! Let's go."

Toronto traffic was not like Regina traffic. Especially not right at 5 p.m. They finally crawled into the parking garage at 6:30, and took the elevator up to the condo, where a new guard was waiting to relieve Emeka. This one was wearing the same immaculate blue suit and black tie and shiny black shoes, but he was taller and just ever-so-slightly skinnier – which still made him look like someone who could eat Wally for breakfast. He had brown skin and brown eyes and a thick black beard.

"What's your name?" Wally asked him.

"Iftekhar Al-Kharafi," the man said.

"Ah." The name had flown by. "Is it all right if I call you Al?"

"No," Iftekhar said.

"Right." *Where does Major get these guys?* Wally wondered. *Thugs 'R' Us?* "Well, um, Iftekhar...did I get it right?...want to come in and watch *Spiderman 3* on the big screen?"

"It is not allowed," Iftekhar said.

Emeka frowned at Wally. "Go inside," he said. He looked at Iftekhar. "Is the pizza here?"

Iftekhar nodded.

Emeka's stern gaze flicked back to Wally. "Have your supper," he said. "Watch your movies. Tomorrow morning I am to take you back to the office for more play testing."

"When will Rex be back?" Wally asked. *And where has he gone?* he wanted to add, but he was pretty sure that would be fruitless.

"*Mister* Major does not provide me with details of his schedule," Emeka said. "I do not know. Go inside now."

"Okay, okay...catch you on the flip side." Wally didn't think he'd ever used that phrase before, but it had the distinct virtue of being annoying. He turned and went into the suite. He would have liked to have locked the door, but he was pretty sure that would have seemed suspicious.

He desperately wanted to head straight into Major's office and continue exploring those mysterious files, but first things first: pizza. And caesar salad. And riblets. And...

Comfortably stuffed, he boxed up what was left of the pizza – not as much as might have been expected, but, *Hey*, he thought, *I'm a teenage boy* – and put it in the giant stainless-steel refrigerator. The pizza had come with a big plastic tumbler of Coke. He took that with him into the media room. He doubted Iftekhar could even hear anything from the hallway, but just in case he could – and just in case he was a secret superhero movie fan – he cued up *Spiderman 3* as promised. As its soundtrack boomed through the speakers, he finally felt safe enough to cross the living room to Major's office and key in the combination code again.

The door opened without any fuss. He slipped in and closed the door behind him. He'd brought the phone from the coffee table and now he slipped it back into its dock.

AVALON got him back into Major's system. He cracked his knuckles – a bad habit he'd developed whenever he sat down at a computer keyboard – and reached for the mouse.

Those secretive files were calling his name, but there was one other thing he wanted to do first: check his email. It had been days since he'd had access to a computer. And it was just possible – just *barely* possible – that Ariane had tried to contact him that way.

Who are you kidding? he thought even as he opened the browser and went to his webmail home page. *She must hate you. You betrayed her and your quest. Sure, it was for her own good. But you'll never convince her of that – especially not while she still has one of the shards of Excalibur.*

Maybe I should have taken both shards, he thought. But then he shook his head. No. He'd known she'd needed the power of the first shard to get across the Atlantic to France. Leaving her in France without it might have stranded her there.

Merlin just needs to get the other shards, he thought. Once he has them, Ariane will have to give up hers, and go back to being an ordinary girl, instead of...whatever she's been turning into.

He typed in his password.

The most recent email leaped out at him.

Suspicious that his sister had been snooping in his computer, Wally had months ago set up a program that would automatically email him whenever his computer was booted up. He'd also deliberately left the computer without password protection, to make it as easy as possible for Flish to trap herself if she came spying.

Rather to his surprise, while she'd lived in the house he'd never once gotten an email indicating she'd turned on his computer when he wasn't there. But now, out of the blue, his system had emailed him, not two minutes before he'd logged onto his webmail home page.

Flish? he thought. *She's moved out. And anyway, she's still in the hospital.* He'd even talked to her on the phone. It hadn't been a particularly pleasant conversation. She knew he was living with Rex Major and was both furious and jealous about it. But he had learned that she would probably be in hospital for another week, and then on crutches for a month after that, and probably a walking cast for a couple of weeks after *that.* There was no way she was in the house.

Mrs. Carson? He shook his head. *She wouldn't even know where the on-off switch was.*

That left only one possibility: only one person he could think of who could have gotten into their locked house without setting off the alarms on the doors and windows, because she didn't have to go through the doors or windows.

Ariane. It has to be Ariane.

And she's in my room.

He winced. He hadn't exactly tidied it up before he'd left. *Well, that's embarrassing.* But he was already searching Major's desktop to see if he had...

There it was. Skype.

Skype would have opened automatically on the computer in his room when it was turned on.

He swallowed...and called his own account.

◂ ▸

Twelve pages of results came up with Ariane's first Google search, and none of the sites looked useful. If Rex Major was travelling anywhere, it hadn't made the news.

She frowned. *He's a famous guy*, she thought. *Recognizable by just about anyone. So what do people do if they see a famous guy somewhere they don't expect to see him?*

Right, she thought. *They put it out on social media.*

She called up Twitter and was just about to run a search for any Tweets mentioning Rex Major when the computer made a chiming noise. She frowned. She knew that tone...

Skype. Someone was Skyping Wally's computer.

She felt a chill. Was Major watching Wally's computer after all?

She found Skype on Wally's machine, and sure enough there was an incoming call...

...from Rex Major.

Her heart suddenly racing, she pushed away from the computer, staring at it as if it might explode. If Major were Skyping her, he knew she was alive. He knew where she was. She couldn't stay!

But then her eyes narrowed. *On the other hand*, she thought, *it's not like he can break in here and kidnap me. And I can be in the pool and away anywhere in the world in seconds. Maybe I should talk to him.*

Maybe I should tell him what I think of him. And Wally.

The first shard burned cold against her skin. She rolled the chair forward again and accepted the call, bracing herself to once more face the age-old sorcerer.

Instead, the screen lit with the freckled face and red hair of Wally Knight, one cheek marked with a red, still-healing scar just above his cheekbone.

Her breath froze in her throat. She couldn't speak, couldn't move. The enormity of emotion she felt on seeing him had seized up every muscle in her body.

Wally didn't seem to have the same problem. "Hello, Ariane," he said. He made a grimace that might have been intended to be a smile, though in practice it mostly made him look like he was going to throw up. "I...um...I'm glad you made it back. From France."

She still couldn't speak. She couldn't believe he had the gall even to talk to her.

The shard of Excalibur burned.

"Ariane," Wally rushed ahead, "I know you must be upset with me, I just want you to know, I did it for your own good –"

"Upset?" The word came out in a kind of strangled squawk. She swallowed, and the next words came easier… and hotter. "Upset? You *betrayed* me. You stole the second shard after I almost died getting it. You gave it Rex Major…to *Merlin*. You gave it to the man who wants to take over the world. You lied to me. You…you…" Three different obscene things to call him vied for the forefront of her brain. In the end she just spluttered.

"Ariane, it's… I…" Wally took a deep breath. "The shards are changing you, Ariane. You can't see it, but I can. They're turning you harder, colder. You…" He touched the scar on his cheek. "You hurt Flish. You hurt me. You're going to hurt yourself. If you'd just give the shard you have to Major…"

"He'd use it to take over the world," Ariane snarled. "To become a dictator. To use Earth's armed forces to attack Faerie. Wally, listen to yourself."

Wally shook his head stubbornly. "Ariane, you're just saying what the Lady of the Lake told you. How do we know we can trust her? So far, Major has never lied to me."

"Really?" Ariane said. "Where is he right now?"

Wally blinked. "I…uh, I don't know."

"For that matter," Ariane said, "where are you? You obviously know where I am." She reached out and grabbed the webcam from where it sat atop his monitor and flashed it around his room. "I'm afraid it's a little the worse for wear."

She shoved the webcam back into place. Wally looked

stricken. "My *Iron Man* poster? You tore up my *Iron Man* poster?"

"You stole the second shard of Excalibur and gave it to the evil wizard Merlin," Ariane said. "One of these things is not like the other."

"He's not..." Wally took a deep breath. "Ariane. He's not evil. He wants to make things better on Earth. And what does it matter whether I know where he is or not? He just had to go out of town on business."

"*What* business?" Ariane opened the browser again, over top of the Skype window, so she didn't have to look at Wally. She typed "#rexmajor" into the "Search Twitter" box.

A line of tweets appeared: and there it was. "Freakin' cool: saw #rexmajor at Glass Field. Geek attack! Dying to know what he's doing here. #computers #technology #ypa."

Glass Field? Ariane thought. *Airport? But what city? That last hashtag...*

"I don't know," Wally's voice said, though she could no longer see him. "He doesn't tell me. He's not just a wizard, you know, he's also got a company to run."

Ariane barely heard him. She was checking to see what the airport code YPA stood for.

It leaped out at her.

Prince Albert Municipal Airport (Glass Field).

Aunt Phyllis!

Forgetting all about Wally, she grabbed the wireless handset on his desk and punched in the number for Aunt Phyllis's cottage. The phone rang – and rang – and rang – and then, just when she thought there'd be no answer...

"Hello?" said a man's voice.

"Who is this?" Ariane said.

"Who is *this*?"

Ariane hesitated. "Wrong number," she said, and hung up.

She stared at the phone as if it were a rabid dog.

"Ariane?" Wally said. "Ariane, what's going on?"

Ariane closed the browser so she could see that hated freckled face again. "You want to know where Rex Major is?" she snarled. "He's in Prince Albert, that's where he is. Practically on top of Emma Lake. He's going after Aunt Phyllis. I think he already has her. So screw you, Wally Knight, and screw your excuses, and your lies. *Rex Major has gone after Aunt Phyllis!*" The sword tip blazed against her side. "And now *I'm* going after *him!*"

She leaped up, the swivel chair flying back from the desk to crash against the wall, then turned and ran out of the room, hearing Wally calling, "Ariane? Ariane!" from the speakers behind her.

Down the stairs, down the short hall to the pool, into the water. She flew north, faster than she had ever travelled before, and exploded from the dark water of Emma Lake right on the shore by Aunt Phyllis's cottage.

There were two men there. They stumbled back as she burst into existence right in front of them, ordering the water from her body with such force that for a moment she was surrounded by fog turned white by the yard light. They reached into their suitcoats, presumably for guns, and she sent them flying with two tendrils of water she tugged from the lake and whipped against their legs. She charged past them.

There was a big black limousine on the road on the other side of the cabin, clouds of exhaust enveloping it in the cold air. Its headlights showed her Aunt Phyllis walking calmly toward it, arm in arm with Rex Major, who was carrying Aunt Phyllis's blue suitcase.

Ariane screamed, *"Aunt Phyllis!"*

Aunt Phyllis glanced her way. Major leaned down and whispered into her ear. She nodded, waved cheerily at Ariane, and then got into the car without the slightest struggle.

Ariane charged forward, but she was too slow. Major got in next to Aunt Phyllis, holding the suitcase on his lap. The door closed. The car backed up, swung around.

Ariane frantically called up water from the lake and hurled it at the limo, but it fell apart, splashing to the road, well behind the car's receding red taillights. But the streetlights showed her the small white rectangle that fluttered out of the car's back window as it sped away.

Ariane ran forward and picked it up from the damp asphalt. It was a business card, with Rex Major's name, the Excalibur Computer Systems logo, and a cell phone number. On the back was scrawled, *Call me.*

Rage roared up into Ariane, some of it hers, much of it from the sword. She whirled to see the two thugs she had upended in the yard hurrying into the old metal boat with the *putt-putting* outboard. They started the motor and headed into the lake. In a moment they'd be out of sight, beyond the reach of the lights on shore...

But they didn't get that far. Ariane reached out and sent an enormous wave hurtling into the boat from the starboard side. The small craft capsized, dumping the men into the water. She clenched her fist, and the wave towered up and split into two tentacles, each capped with a sword of ice. She started to bring the blades down on the struggling men...

...and then realized what she was about to do. She gasped and relaxed, letting the tendrils and ice-blades fall apart. The men had found their feet in the still-shallow water and were making a beeline for the shore, albeit an angled beeline that insured they got as far away from her as possible as fast as possible.

I wanted to kill them, she thought, *feeling a little sick. I was* going *to kill them.*

A thing of war, the Lady had called the sword.

But maybe I'm in a war, she thought. Would the time

come when she wouldn't hold back from the violence the sword was always urging her to commit?

She looked down at Major's business card. If the sword urged violence on Merlin, she thought she'd be *happy* to submit. He intended to use Ariane's aunt as a hostage, to force Ariane to give up her shard. He'd threaten to hurt Aunt Phyllis, even kill her, unless Ariane surrendered.

It had worked for him once before, after all. Major's threat to kill Wally had convinced her to give him the first shard of the sword in Yellowknife, though they'd later stolen it back.

Call me, she read again on the card.

It's a trap, she told herself.

Of course it's a trap, she replied.

And she didn't see any other option but to walk right into it.

The front door to Aunt Phyllis's cabin stood open, and that, as much as anything else she'd seen, convinced Ariane that Major must have used his Voice of Command on her aunt. There was no way, if her aunt had been in her right mind, she would have left her front door open and unlocked, even if she was at home. Especially not this late in the season when most of the cabins were empty and "anyone might come wandering by."

As anyone certainly had.

Ariane took a deep breath. Then she went into the cabin, picked up the handset of the old black rotary telephone, and dialed the number on the card.

CHAPTER FIVE

AWKWARD CONVERSATIONS

WALLY STARED AT THE SCREEN, still showing his bedroom in Regina. *Rex Major is in Prince Albert? He's going after Aunt Phyllis?*

He called up Twitter and did his own search. Sure enough, someone had seen Major at the Prince Albert airport.

He could be there for other reasons, he thought. *Mining. Logging. Fishing...don't jump to conclusions. He hasn't lied to you yet. He'll tell you why he was there.*

But...

He sighed. The file folders on Major's computer were still calling to him, but he shoved back from the desk and went to his own room. In his backpack there was a leather pouch containing his passport, a few left-over Euros – and a card Aunt Phyllis had given him before they left her house in Regina for Chamberlain, where he and Ariane had parted ways with her before heading to France, he by jet, Ariane by cloud-jumping. The card had Aunt Phyllis's phone number in Emma Lake written on it in green ink.

He picked up the handset in his room and dialed the number.

The phone rang, over and over. On the eighth ring, he heard it picked up. "Hello?" said a voice.

A *man's* voice.

Just in time, Wally thought to deepen and coarsen his own. "May I speak to Phyllis Forsythe, please?"

A pause. "She's not available. Can I take a message?"

Wally ignored that. "Then can I speak to Rex Major?" he growled.

A much longer pause. "Who is this?"

Wally disconnected, swearing. Ariane had been telling the truth. Rex Major had grabbed Aunt Phyllis. He was going to hold her hostage to force Ariane to give him the first shard. It was the only thing that made sense.

He doesn't know I know, Wally thought. *And that means it's the perfect test for his promise he'll always tell me the truth.* He stared at the phone. *He's supposed to call me this evening. I'll see what he says. And then...*

He swallowed. He was beginning to think he'd made a terrible, terrible mistake. And if he had – with a guard on the door, no money, and nobody to turn to for help – he didn't see a thing he could do about it.

◀ ▶

Ariane held the black Bakelite handset as if it were a poisonous snake that might whip around and sink its fangs into her wrist at any moment. But of course the snake was on the other end of the line...and answered after two rings.

"Hello, Ariane," Rex Major said.

She didn't bother asking how he knew it was her. "What have you done with Aunt Phyllis?" she snarled, the shard of Excalibur burning against her skin and filling her with righteous anger.

"She's safe," Major said. "Would you like to talk to her?"

Ariane blinked. "I can?"

"Of course." Fumbling sounds on the other end, then, "Here you go, Phyllis."

"Thanks, Rex," Ariane heard Aunt Phyllis say. Then her aunt was on the phone. "Hello, dear. How nice to hear your voice. How is your vacation?"

Dumbfounded, it took Ariane a moment to respond. "Vacation?"

"Rex...Mr. Major...tells me you're camping with some friends. That sounds like fun."

"No, Aunt Phyllis," Ariane said, bewildered. "I'm at your cabin at Emma Lake. Where you were taken from. Like, ten minutes ago. You saw me."

"Well, I must say it's so nice to hear that you're doing things with other friends than just Wally," Aunt Phyllis went on as if she hadn't spoken – or as if she had said something completely different than she really had. "He's a nice boy, don't get me wrong, but you need to make more friends."

"Aunt Phyllis," Ariane said, speaking very slowly and distinctly, "you are a hostage. Rex Major has kidnapped you. He's using you to get the shards of Excalibur. You know all that, don't you?"

"That does sound delightful," Aunt Phyllis said, then, "Oh! Rex wants to talk to you again. Stay warm, dear, and I'll see you soon."

And just like that, she was gone.

Major came back on the line. "I told you she was fine," he said.

"Fine?" Ariane exploded. "She's not fine! You've... brainwashed her, or something. She didn't hear a word I said."

"She heard you," Major said calmly. "Well, she heard your voice. The words she came up with herself, to match the Commands I gave her. She is convinced I'm an old family friend, that I've invited her to stay with me for a few days, and she is delighted to do so."

"You've twisted her mind," Ariane said, feeling sick. "You're a monster."

"Hardly," Major said, voice sharpening. "I have done nothing to hurt her. I take no pleasure in causing people pain, Ariane. But my needs are great and my ultimate goals, the liberation of an entire world – my world! – and the return of magic in all its power to this one, outweigh ordinary empathy for others."

"That's inhuman."

Major laughed. "You mean that as an insult, I suppose. But it's a simple statement of fact. Yes, I'm inhuman…because I'm not human. I'm a…" He chuckled again. "Fairy."

"I'm sticking with *monster*," Ariane said. "So let me guess. You want me to give you the first shard in exchange for Aunt Phyllis's life."

"Oh, no," Major said. "Quite the contrary. I want you to meet with me…so I can give you the second shard."

Ariane pulled the handset away from her ear, stared at it a moment, then put it back. "What?"

"I want to give you the second shard. So you'll have both of them again."

"*Why?*"

"Can't tell you that over the phone, I'm afraid."

Ariane said nothing for a moment, chewing her lower lip. *It's a trick of some kind*, she thought. *It has to be.*

But what choice did she have? Major had Aunt Phyllis. Ariane had to try to get her back.

I've got the magic of the Lady of the Lake, she thought. *I'm powerful. I can do this.*

But there was one other thing she could do first. Something that might give her some protection Merlin hadn't counted on.

Mind made up, she said, "All right. How do I find you?"

"You don't," Major said. "You stay put. I'll send my limo back. It will bring you to me. I have to arrange a few things first, of course, so let's say...first thing in the morning. You have a lovely night in Aunt Phyllis's cabin, and I'll send a car around at 9 a.m." Even over the phone, she could tell he was smiling. "I look forward to seeing you again."

"The feeling is not mutual," Ariane said, and slammed the handset down into its cradle. *I'll say one thing for the old phones*, she thought, staring at it. *It's way more satisfying hanging up on someone that way then pushing a virtual button on a smartphone screen.*

She had all night. Plenty of time.

She rushed out, waded into the lake, and let the water suck her down.

◄◄ ►►

Rex Major winced as the crash of Ariane's hang-up spiked his ear, but smiled all the same as the limo rolled along the road toward Prince Albert. *That went well*, he thought. Now that he had received the expected phone call from Ariane, he could make the promised phone call to Wally Knight. He glanced at Aunt Phyllis, debating whether he needed to Command her to not hear his end of that talk. He decided it was unnecessary. She was so muddled and delusional thanks to the Commands he had already given her she probably wouldn't even register it, and if she did, she'd imagine it as something completely different from reality.

Ariane had accused him of twisting the old lady's mind, but he hadn't twisted anything. Her mind was fine. In fact, it was working overtime, imposing its own dream-like layer of alternate reality on the world around it in obedience to his Command. Once he lifted the Commands...*if* he lifted them, *if* Ariane cooperated...she would return to normal, albeit with a certain amount of confusion as to what had been real and what had been imagined during the time she was under his spell.

He couldn't Command Wally, because he was the heir of King Arthur – or so Major strongly suspected. He couldn't Command Ariane, because she was the Lady of the Lake. But he *could* Command his guards, and, it turned out, he could Command Phyllis Forsythe.

He rubbed his temple with the heel of his right hand. He had a deuce of a headache, though. There were several Commands keeping Phyllis happily ensconced in her pleasant dream world. He had used more of his meagre store of magic than he liked to at any one time. *But needs must*, he thought.

He dialed the number of his Toronto condo. He was applying the mushroom principle when it came to Wally: keep him in the dark and feed him crap. There was no need for Wally to know anything about what was happening here in Prince Albert. In fact, the less he knew, the better. He'd never understand about Phyllis.

The phone rang several times before anyone answered. "Hello?" said Wally's light tenor.

"Hi, Wally," Major said. "What are you doing?"

"Just finished watching a movie," Wally said. "I asked the guard to join me but he didn't seem interested in *Spiderman 3*."

Major laughed. "Don't take it personally. I would have fired him if he had." He glanced out at the passing trees, barely glimpsed in the spill from the headlights. "I'm just sitting on the terrace of my hotel in Vancouver, looking out at the harbour," he said. "Sipping wine and wishing I didn't have more meetings tomorrow."

"Sounds nice," Wally said, unenthusiastically.

"Feeling cooped up?" Major said. "Even after play-testing the King Arthur game all day?"

"A little," Wally said.

"Well, I've arranged for you to start fencing lessons to-morrow," Major said. "And your tutor will be coming in on Monday. I'll try to keep you from being bored."

"We don't even know if Ariane is alive," Wally said, sounding more like a stereotypical sullen teen than Major had ever heard him. "Why do I have to stay cooped up?" His voice tightened. "Or have you heard something? Is she alive?"

"I still don't know," Major lied, keeping his own voice warm and sympathetic. "I'm sorry, Wally. I really need you to stay safe. We don't know what she'll do if she is alive, with the sword driving her. You hurt her far more than your sister did, and you know what she did to *her*."

"Yeah," Wally said. "I know." A pause. "When will you be coming back?"

"I'm here for one more day, at least," Major said. "Things are a bit up in the air after that. Depends on what happens in my next meeting." It always pleased Merlin when he could deceive while actually telling the truth. It didn't happen all that often. "If things go well, I may have to take another trip after that...could be over-seas." *Depending on where the third shard is.* "I'll keep you posted." *I mean, I'll lie to you on a regular basis.*

"All right," Wally said. "Guess there's nothing I can do but cue up another movie."

"Sorry," Major said. "I'll make it up to you when I get back...I think I'm about ready to tell you what I've dis-covered about you. But not over the phone. In person." *That'll keep him quiet*, he thought.

"All right," Wally said again. "Goodbye."

"Goodbye."

Wally hung up much more quietly than Ariane had.

Major pocketed his cell phone and turned back to Phyllis. "It's a very scenic drive, isn't it?" she said, a remark that came entirely out of her own self-generated delusions, since it was almost pitch dark outside. "I can't thank you enough for inviting me to visit."

"Believe me," Rex Major said, "the pleasure is all mine."

◀◀ ▶▶

Wally stared at the phone handset he had just put down, then at the computer screen. *That tears it*, he thought savagely. *Wally Knight, you're an idiot.* He'd let himself be sucked in by smooth words and vague promises of greatness. He'd betrayed his best friend while telling himself it was for her own good…heck, for the good of the whole world. He'd really thought Rex Major – *Merlin*, the ancient sorcerer who once manipulated all of Camelot from behind Arthur's throne – had been telling him the truth, had Ariane's best interests at heart, had *his* best interests at heart, had *Earth's* best interests at heart, instead of being ruthlessly focused on his own dreams of conquest and "liberation."

Like I said. You're an idiot.

It wasn't just the lying phone call from Major that had convinced him of that inconvenient truth. It was also the photo he had opened on the man's computer just before the phone rang.

It wasn't a very good photo. It wasn't in colour, it was only vaguely in focus, and the composition left a lot to be desired. But it wasn't the photo itself but the person it showed that had hit Wally like a punch to the stomach.

The photo was a single frame from a cheap security camera in a convenience store. It showed the sales counter, at the odd angle that seemed strangely familiar to Wally from countless YouTube and Crime Stopper videos of robberies and customer confrontations. There was a male clerk at the counter, who had apparently just served a woman wearing a hooded coat who, on turning away, had lifted her head just enough for the camera to capture her face.

Wally had never seen her before. But someone had helpfully captioned the photo in block letters at the bottom. *EMILY FORSYTHE. 98% CONFIDENCE. STOP-N-RUN CONVENIENCE STORE. CARLYLE, SASKATCHEWAN.* There followed a date.

The photo had been taken a little over six weeks earlier.

The photo told Wally two things: Ariane's mother was alive – and Major was looking for her.

Major hadn't told Wally about that. He certainly hadn't told Ariane. And Wally could think of only one reason Major would even be interested in Ariane's mother: to turn her into a hostage. Just as he'd apparently done with Aunt Phyllis. All to force Ariane to give up her quest and surrender the shards of Excalibur to him.

I've got to tell Ariane, Wally thought. *I've got to help her find her mother. I've got to get away from Rex Major. I've got to...*

I've got to make up for being an idiot.

He sighed. Regrets were all very well. Actually doing anything to make right what he had done wrong was likely to prove seriously difficult. He didn't even know exactly where Major was, aside from Prince Albert.

But maybe I can find out, he thought. He opened Major's email program.

There was no guarantee, of course, that Major would have his business email forwarded to his home computer, or that the messages he sent from his cell phone would be copied to it – but Wally would have been willing to bet on it. And he would have won, because there were the messages Major had been sending and receiving while he was away, plain as day. And one of them told Wally exactly what he wanted to know. The email address was frank@ochranasecurity.com.

Mr. Major, it read, *We have a secure location for you, fitting the specifications you provided. It's a gravel quarry some twenty kilometres southeast of Prince Albert. The quarry has been closed for three months due to financial difficulties. We have been hired to provide site security, and thus have access. We have placed a camper in the middle of the quarry floor. As you specified, there are no bodies of water within two kilometres and no running water at the site. Please advise if this will meet your needs. Frank.*

To which Major had simply replied, *Perfect. Will call with details.*

I wonder, Wally thought, staring at that email, *how far rescuing Aunt Phyllis from Rex Major would go toward making up for my betrayal?*

Realistically, maybe not very far. But whether it helped Ariane forgive him or not, he owed it to Aunt Phyllis to free her from Major if he could. The question was, could he?

He stared at Major's computer. Then he started opening other files. He clicked over to a few websites. He started to smile.

Oh, he could do it.

The smile faded.

Provided, of course, that he could get past the guard at the door. But he even had a plan for that.

First, though...

He settled to work on the computer in earnest.

CHAPTER SIX

THE DREAMING HOSTAGE

FIVE MINUTES BEFORE THE LIMO WAS DUE, Ariane emerged from Aunt Phyllis's cabin into the frosty November air. There had been a skiff of snow overnight, just enough to highlight the ground with white. She yawned. She'd been busy during the first part of the night and then had had trouble sleeping. It felt odd not to have the first shard of Excalibur strapped to her side, but even though she'd left it far away, she could feel it in her thoughts as always. It was still "hers." Somehow, it knew it hadn't been abandoned.

She didn't think she could have called on its power even if it weren't blocked by the second shard's being in Merlin's grasp. It felt too distant for that. But she could "hear" it, just as she had heard the second shard while she had had the first, and just as she was sure she could hear the third shard if only Wally hadn't...

Anger flared in her again at the thought of Wally. *That* hadn't changed with leaving the sword behind, either. Its anger still fuelled her own. *I'll never forgive him for what he did*, she thought. *Never. He betrayed me. He betrayed Aunt Phyllis. And now Major has her.*

The next time I see him...

I should have done more than trash his room, she thought. *I should have burned down his house.*

A quiet, rather fearful part of her objected to that thought, but she shoved it aside with the force of Excalibur's righteous anger and stood, arms folded, glaring at the road, waiting for the limo.

It appeared a minute later, making a U-turn and pulling up right beside her. She opened the door and got in beside the driver, who said "Buckle up," and then didn't say another word for the rest of the drive.

They started off as though heading for Prince Albert, but before they got to the city the limo turned onto a side road that led through the forest. Ariane frowned. No water anywhere around them that she could sense. Major wasn't taking any chances.

After a few more minutes the trees thinned and they came to the edge of a giant pit, a quarry of some kind, piles of loose stone all around the edges. The limo nosed down a narrow track that slanted down one wall of the pit to the snow-dusted gravel of the bottom. In the very middle of the pit sat a camper, an old-fashioned cream-and-brown Winnebago. A second vehicle was parked next to it, an SUV as black as the limo. On the side a decal read *OCHRANA SECURITY* in big silver block letters, and *Private Protection Since 1976* in a smaller, cursive font. Two men in black suits stood guard on either side of the door to the construction trailer. They had the same no-nonsense attitude as her driver – and the same massive builds.

Rex Major making sure nobody directly connects anything he does out here with Excalibur Computer Systems, Ariane thought.

They pulled up next to the trailer. One of the guards strode forward and opened the door, then extended a hand. Ariane ignored it and climbed out on her own. He lowered his hand. "Rex Major is expecting you," he said. "This way."

"I know the way," Ariane said. "It's right in front of me. It's not like I can get lost." She strode past him before he could react, feet crunching in snow and gravel, and up to the trailer door. Jerking it open, she stepped inside, the camper rocking slightly beneath her weight. "I'm here," she snapped. "What do you want?"

Rex Major sat on a loveseat-sized couch the colour of old mustard, watching a tiny black-and-white TV on a shelf on the opposite wall. Aunt Phyllis sat next to him. Both of their heads turned as the door opened. "Ariane!" Aunt Phyllis said with a bright smile. "How nice of you to join us!" She looked at Major. "Rex," she said, waggling a finger at him. "You didn't tell me you'd invited Ariane, too."

"I wanted it to be a surprise, Phyllis," Major said with an indulgent chuckle. And then his voice altered, becoming strangely resonant and compelling. "Take a nap."

Immediately Aunt Phyllis yawned, closed her eyes, and slumped down where she sat.

Ariane's fists clenched. "Leave her alone!"

"Or what?" Major said, unruffled. "You're unarmed. You have no water to draw on. There is nothing you can do to me here."

"There's nothing you can do to me, either," Ariane snarled. "You can't kill me. You can't take the first shard from me by force. I have to give it to you willingly. And guess what? I didn't bring it with me. It's hidden where you'll never find it."

"I told you," Major said, "that I don't want you to give me the first shard. I want to give *you* the second. Didn't you believe me?"

"Of course I didn't –"

But then, to her utter shock, Major reached into his coat pocket and drew out the second shard of Excalibur.

It looked just as she remembered it: broken at both ends, pitted but not rusted. And the most shocking thing was that she hadn't even known she was in the same room with it. Before, in France, even after Wally had taken it from her, she'd been able to tell where it was. Now...it was like she was looking at any ordinary piece of metal.

Major laughed again. "I see I've surprised you," he said. The ruby stud in his right ear glinted as he glanced down at the shard in his hand. "It's true I have little enough power in this world at the moment," he said, "but that is not the same as no power at all." He jerked his head at the old woman. "As your snoring relative proves." He held up the shard. "I have power enough to cloak the presence of this shard from you if it is on my person."

"So what," Ariane said, trying to sound hard and confident. "There's a giant pile of junk that used to be a mining shovel in the Northwest Territories that shows the kind of power *I* have."

Major's eyes narrowed just a fraction at that. *A hit, a palpable hit*, she thought with more than a little pleasure.

But Major took a breath and stepped forward. "A useless discussion," he said. "Let us advance to the point." He held out the second shard. "Take it. It's yours."

At first Ariane couldn't even make sense of the words. Even when she did, she made no move to take the shard. "Is this some kind of trick?"

"Does it look like a trick?" Major said. He stretched his hand out farther. "Please, I insist. Take the second shard. I give it to you freely."

Ariane hesitated a moment longer, then, as though trying to grab a snake before it could turn and bite her, seized the shard. The instant she touched it she heard its song as she should have all along, vibrant, excited. Not for the first time she felt the sword *knew* she was the heir of the one who had had it forged in Faerie, and approved of her touch.

"Now that that's done," Major said, "let's talk."

"What's to stop me from just turning and walking out with it?" Ariane said.

Major glanced at Aunt Phyllis. "Did you miss the part where I kidnapped your aunt and put her under a magic spell? Just like in the old fairy tales?" He smiled. "I wrote some of those, you know. The original versions. The really *dark* ones. I was pleased upon awakening in the twentieth century to discover many of them have been told for centuries." The smile faded. "Although Walt Disney has a lot to answer for." Then the smile returned. "I assure you, however, that neither your kiss nor the kiss of a handsome prince will break *that* spell." He jerked a thumb at Aunt Phyllis.

Ariane clenched her hand on the shard. "So what's all this about?"

"You have the first two shards now," Major said. "That should make it easy for you to hear the third. I want you to locate it. Then you're going to lead me to it, and help me retrieve it, if it is hidden in water, as it almost certainly is. And once we have it, you will give all three shards to me." He glanced at Aunt Phyllis again. "Or Sleeping Beauty...dies."

Ariane's heart pounded. She knew he wasn't bluffing. "If you kill her, I'll never give you the shards."

He shrugged. "So what? Her only value to me is as a hostage. If she's not even any good to me as a hostage, I might as well kill her so she can't interfere in any other way...and to punish you."

"Wally would never forgive you."

"Wally would never know I had anything to do with it," Major said. "Wally is living in luxury in Toronto, having the time of his life playing a next-generation virtual-reality game my company has under development. I've told him he's important to my plans. Which he is. But only," and he smiled again, though it had more in common with the grimace of a death's head than ordinary human amusement, "as long as I still have a chance of getting all five shards. If I were to lose that capability – because, for example, you decided to flee with the shards once we had found the third – then his potential for greatness in my service would become instead a potential for greatness in yours, and I would have no choice but to execute him, too."

"This is the twenty-first century," Ariane said desperately. "You can't just kill people on a whim like you did in…whenever it was."

"Have you watched the news recently?" Major said. "Of *course* I can. In fact it's *easier* today than it was in Arthur's day. More people. More ways to die. More ways to cover up who really killed them." His voice hardened. "Enough of this. Do it. Find the shard. Tell me where it is. And then we'll see about going there…together."

Ariane had never felt so helpless. "I don't have the first shard with me."

"I'm not surprised," Major said. "But that shouldn't have any effect on your ability to find the third, now that my possession of the second is no longer interfering with it. *Listen.*"

Ariane closed her eyes and concentrated. And almost at once, she heard it – like the first two, but subtly different, and far, far away. "It's…south," she said, speaking almost without realizing she was doing so. "Very far south. And…west. Or is it east?" She frowned. "No, west. But also very, very far." She opened her eyes. "That's the best I can do," she said desperately. "It's not like a GPS. It's just a…a…sense." She had been going to say *song*.

"Very far south. And west. Farther than France?"

She nodded. "Much farther."

"Could be Asia, but if it's really far south..." He shrugged. "Well, we'll track it down. We'll start in Australia and work out from there."

Ariane stared at him. "Australia? You're taking me to Australia?"

"I already explained my plan," Major said. "Weren't you listening?"

"But what about Aunt Phyllis?"

"Aunt Phyllis," Major said, "will stay here. Continuing to believe that she is an honoured guest living, like Wally, in the lap of luxury. That way, when we find the third shard, there will be no opportunity for you to do anything to rescue her. And if you do not then immediately give me the two shards you have – and take me to wherever you have hidden the first – she will suffer for it. Are you perfectly clear on the plan now?"

Ariane nodded, feeling sick to her stomach. There was no way she could see to prevent Major's plan from working. He held all the cards, and they were all aces. "Yes," she whispered.

"Good." Major went to the door, opened it, and stuck his head outside. "We'll need a ride to my hotel," he said. "The old woman will stay here. Take good care of her."

"Yes, sir," the goon outside said briskly.

Major pulled his head back inside. "Let's go, Ariane," he said. "We have a long journey ahead of us. I will retrieve my belongings from the hotel and talk to my pilot. Then I'll need to make some phone calls and conduct other business. It will be some hours yet, but never fear, we'll be on our way before the day is out."

Stomach churning, still clutching the second shard of Excalibur in her hand and hearing the call of the third in her head, she stepped out into the chill air.

CHAPTER SEVEN

ARRIVALS AND DEPARTURES

THE FIREPLACE POKER WASN'T SHAPED like a sword, and it wasn't weighted or balanced like a sword, but Wally thought – or at least devoutly hoped – it would serve. He stood just inside the condo's main front door. He'd spent a restless night reviewing his plans, then had gotten up early, figuring if he were going to make a break for it, it had to be before he was hauled off to play the King Arthur game again...and hoping the element of surprise might be greater if he acted while the guard might expect him to still be sleeping.

He'd had breakfast (he hadn't bothered to clean up), pulled on his backpack, reviewed his plans one more time, and double-checked to make sure he had erased all signs of his presence on Major's computer. Not that he could keep secret *everything* he had done on the machine. Eventually, for example, Major would notice the rather large withdrawal of money from his chequing account. At some point he might even discover the new "Rex Major" email account Wally had set up that Wally had the password to and he didn't. But it should all remain a secret long enough for him to get to Prince Albert and rescue Aunt Phyllis.

And, Wally hoped, find out where Major had gone in pursuit of the third shard – and maybe even where Ariane was.

But first he had to get by…whomever was in the hallway.

He wasn't actually sure. It could be Emeka. It could be Iftekhar. It could be some minion he hadn't met yet.

He took a deep breath. *Okay*, he thought. *This always works in movies.*

"Help!" he screamed, voice breaking. "Help! Help! Help!" Not the most original dialogue, but short and to the point.

He heard footsteps running toward the door. It swung inward. Iftekhar rushed in, gun in hand. Wally dodged around him and dashed down the hall toward the elevator, slamming the door behind him. He couldn't lock it, but it would slow the guard.

He hoped.

Not very much, it seemed. It was already swinging open.

Wally pounded on the button of the elevator, even though he knew pushing it over and over again did nothing to make it come faster. Iftekhar was coming. The elevator wasn't there. He turned frantically and held the poker *en garde*. Iftekhar slowed. "What are you doing?" he said. He sounded more puzzled than anything else. He had holstered his gun. "Why did you call for help?"

"I'm escaping," Wally said.

Iftekhar frowned. "Escaping? Escaping from where?"

"From here," Wally said. "From you."

Iftekhar's frown deepened. "I don't understand."

"You're holding me prisoner here. I don't want to be a prisoner."

"I am not holding you prisoner. I am protecting you."

Wally glanced up at the elevator. Twenty floors to go.

"Protecting me from what? Or who?" He paused. "Um...I mean, whom?"

Iftekhar shrugged. "I do not know. I have just been ordered to protect you."

"Well, you can stop."

"No. I cannot. I must protect you. That means you cannot leave."

"But I am leaving."

"Then I will stop you."

"Then you are holding me prisoner."

"No, I am protecting you."

Ten floors.

"Either way, I'm leaving."

Iftekhar sighed. "I don't want to hurt you."

"I don't want to hurt you."

Iftekhar laughed. "You won't."

Wally hefted the poker. "I might."

The elevator pinged. The doors slid open. Iftekhar lunged. Wally, without even thinking, parried his outstretched arm, spun and struck with the poker. It thudded against Iftekhar's head. The man dropped like a stone. Wally had a horrified glimpse of blood starting to pool beneath his skull before the elevator door slid shut.

Wally backed up against the back wall of the elevator, shaking. He hadn't meant to hurt Iftekhar. He didn't even know how he'd done what he did. The poker had almost had a life of its own, as though it were wielding him instead of him wielding it.

It was the whole lousy-fencer-to-Western-Canada-competitor phenomenon all over again. It had to have something to do with whatever secret Major was keeping from him.

Guess I'll never know what that is after this, he thought.

And then he thought, with a sense of dread, *Did I just kill a man? Did I kill him?*

He dropped the poker. It had blood on it. It looked like a murder weapon. Maybe it was. Maybe he was a murderer.

Even if he wasn't – even if he'd just given the guy a concussion – *he'd given a guy a concussion.* Concussions could be serious. He should know. And Iftekhar had been bleeding. A lot. What if he bled to death?

I've got to get help for him, Wally thought. *But I've got to get out of here, too. I've got a plane to catch. Aunt Phyllis has no one else.*

When the elevator had started sinking it had felt as if he'd left his stomach behind. It still hadn't caught up.

How could I do that to him? he thought. *I've never hurt anyone before. I've never* wanted *to hurt anyone before...well, not badly,* honesty forced him to add. There had been a time or two when Flish –

His mind was skittering away from what he had done. He forced it back on track. *That wasn't me. That was... someone else. That was...*

And then it hit him, as hard as he had hit Iftekhar.

That was *the sword.* That was Excalibur. That was the same force that had changed Ariane, fuelled her anger to the point she had put Flish in the hospital.

But I'm not the Lady of the Lake! he cried to himself.

Yet he *was* something special. At least Major – *Merlin* – thought so. The Lady had thought so, too. "I wonder if Merlin..." she'd said when he'd met her in Wascana Lake. Wondered if Merlin what? Knew the truth about *him?*

And Ariane had said that the first two shards of Excalibur hadn't wanted to play together...until he'd touched them. Then they'd sung in perfect harmony. He hadn't heard it. He hadn't heard anything. But just like Ariane, he had held the shards of Excalibur. The first, when that was all they had. The second, when he had taken it to Merlin. And both together in the hotel room. And somehow, whatever that sword truly was, it had called out to whatever *he* truly was.

He had thought that by betraying Ariane and stealing the second shard he was saving her from the sword's violent influence. But who would save *him*?

He swallowed hard. Then the elevator reached the garage level and the door opened. Wally snatched up the poker and dashed out. He looked around hurriedly, saw a garbage can just outside the elevator hallway, and threw the poker into it. The police would surely find it there, but he hoped to be long gone.

He couldn't leave Iftekhar bleeding and unconscious. The man needed an ambulance, right away. He got back on the elevator, rode it up to the lobby, hurried over to the security desk. The guard looked up at him, frowned. "Who are you?"

"Wal..." Wally stopped just in time. "Wallace Gromit," he said in a panic, and then winced. But apparently the guard was not an aficionado of stop-motion animation.

"You look like you've seen a ghost, Wallace," the guard said.

"Man...hurt," Wally said, deciding to stick with the bunny-in-the-headlights approach. "Rex...Rex Major's floor."

"What?" The guard jumped up. "What kind of injury?"

"Head injury," Wally said. "He fell. Blood everywhere."

The guard ran for the elevators. Wally turned and dashed toward the front door. The guard shouted after him, but Wally was already on the street. Five minutes later he was on the subway. A few random back-and-forths on the subway and a dash through the "underground city," which sprawled beneath Toronto's downtown like an endless shopping mall, and he was pretty sure he'd lost any pursuers. Also himself, but he could always find himself again.

He sat in a coffee shop, had a latte, and caught his breath. He had no idea how long word would take to get to Rex Major that his guard was injured and Wally was gone. He didn't even know how Major would interpret that. Would he think Wally was kidnapped? Wally snorted. *Who would kidnap me?*

No, Major would figure out right away what Wally had done. But he might not guess *why*. So what would he do?

Wally didn't know. All he could do was press on with his plan…and hope Major couldn't figure out where he was headed.

He glanced at his watch. His Air Canada flight to Saskatoon left at 12:05 Toronto time and arrived at 2:40 Saskatoon time, leaving him with just over half an hour to grab the 3:15 Transwest Airlines flight from there to Prince Albert. He'd be in Prince Albert with maybe an hour of daylight left to try to do something about Aunt Phyllis.

It was time to get to the airport.

First, though…

There was an ATM not far from where he sat. He took out his bank card and withdrew $1,000 – his limit. It barely scratched the surface of the money he'd transferred from Major's account, but just in case Major found out about that and somehow stopped the transaction, he thought he'd better draw out as much as he could.

Feeling rather naked with that much cash on him, even though no one had been nearby when he'd taken it out and even though he immediately hid it in his backpack, he hurried off to the nearest exit to street level. Emerging on Bloor, he flagged down a taxi. A taxi ride to the airport was expensive, but it wasn't like he didn't have the money.

He couldn't hide his identity while flying, and he knew Major's magic could conceivably be monitoring every airline transaction, but on the other hand, when he had bought the tickets, Major hadn't had any reason to be concerned that Wally might be flying somewhere. Wally hoped that was enough to keep him in the dark.

Check-in and boarding went smoothly. Wally settled back in his seat on the Air Canada jet and closed his eyes. A little over three hours to Saskatoon, and he hadn't slept well the night before. He intended to make up for it.

But after ten futile minutes he opened his eyes again and sighed. *Stupid brain*, he thought. *Quit thinking.*

But it didn't pay him any attention. As he winged his way west, the same three thoughts kept spinning around in his head like hyperactive puppies chasing their tails. *Where is Major? Where is Ariane? And where is the third shard?*

And just like those tail-chasing canines, all he got was dizzy.

So he locked them in a metaphorical kennel and decided to spend his time more productively: figuring out how he was going to rescue Aunt Phyllis. By the time the plane touched down in Saskatoon, he had a pretty good idea. It all depended on Major still being blissfully unaware that his email had been hacked, of course – if you could call it hacking when he'd been sitting at Major's own computer when he'd done it. In any event, Wally thought there was a pretty good chance Major still didn't know about it. Even if Major had been informed by now that Wally had flown the coop – and sorry though he was for what he had done to Iftekhar, he rather hoped the man was still in no condition to answer questions, because the longer he remained incommunicado, the longer Major would remain in the dark – Major had no reason to think Wally had managed to break into his office and access his computer.

More likely he'd think Wally had just gone stir crazy, had somehow managed to hurt Iftekhar, and then had run in panic. Which meant he would most likely think Wally was still in Toronto. The last place he would expect him to be was in Prince Albert, trying to rescue Aunt Phyllis.

Which meant Wally's mad scheme to do so just might have a chance.

◄◄ ►►

Late in the afternoon, Ariane rode in silence in the back of the limo as it rolled toward the Prince Albert airport. Rex Major sat in the front next to the driver, talking quietly into his phone, leaving her with nothing to do but stare out the window and try to figure out something, anything, she could do to thwart Major's well-laid plans.

As she had all day, she came up dry. *Literally*, she thought. Oh, they had passed water en route to the airport, but it zipped by too fast for her to do anything with it even if she'd had an idea. Force the car off the road and then slip away into a handy stream? Major would still have Aunt Phyllis.

Form the water into a sword of ice and kill him where he sat?

She shuddered. The fact she'd even thought of that scared her. The fact she thought the sword would entirely *approve* of that scared her *more*. She had the horrible feeling that if she ever gave in to the sword's most bloodthirsty urges, there would be no going back. She would begin to use the sword as it wanted to be used – or it would use her – and then how would she be any better than Merlin?

She folded her arms and sat in unhappy silence for the rest of the ride.

From the outside, the terminal looked more like a bus depot than what she thought of as an airport building, although a little farther off stood a more airporty structure, with a small control tower attached.

But they drove right past the terminal, heading to a hangar. "My pilot is ready to go," Major said over his shoulder to Ariane. "The plane is fully fuelled and he's already filed the flight plan. I'd love to fly directly to Honolulu and then head on to Sydney...but you don't have a passport with you, do you?"

"My passport is somewhere at the bottom of that cave in France," Ariane said, heart leaping with sudden hope. *It takes weeks to get a passport. I'll have time to figure out some way to –*

Major nodded. "So we go to Vancouver first. We get you a replacement passport. *Then* we'll fly to Hawaii. I have some business there anyway. Then on to Sydney. We'll home in on the third shard from there...unless you get a better idea of its location before we get there."

Ariane said nothing.

They pulled up to the hanger. Major got out, came around, and opened the door for her. She climbed sullenly out, not looking at him. He sighed. "You might as well enjoy the trip," he said. "Not many fifteen-year-olds get to take a private jet to Vancouver, Honolulu, and Sydney."

"Not many fifteen-year-olds get kidnapped by a thousand-year-old sorcerer," Ariane snapped.

Major laughed. "I know. Makes you doubly lucky, doesn't it?"

He offered her his arm. She gave him what she hoped was a withering look, but he remained disappointingly unwithered. *In movies, magically preserved monsters always crumble into dust before the final credits*, she thought savagely. *If only I had a spell to make that happen to* him.

This time she didn't berate herself for her bloodthirstiness. *That* bit of rage she was pretty certain had nothing to do with the sword. Rex Major was threatening Aunt Phyllis. She didn't need any magical boost to feel angry about *that*.

The jet Major led her to looked only slightly smaller than the Transwest Airlines commercial turboprop plane that had just landed and was pulling up to the terminal. The jet had the Excalibur Computer Systems logo on it. Ariane glanced around at the Transwest Airlines plane, hoping someone on board would look out at and think there was something strange about a teenage girl getting aboard a corporate jet with an older man, but realistically, why would they? He could be her father, after all.

Someone might recognize the logo, though. Someone might even recognize Rex Major.

Maybe Wally will...

She cut that thought off. Old habits died hard. Yes, Wally might see a Tweeted photo of the jet, or of her – and wouldn't care. He wanted Major to do whatever he was doing. *He's not on my side anymore*, she reminded herself. *He's not my friend. He's my enemy. Like Merlin.*

I have no friends.

I have no allies – except Aunt Phyllis, and she's more of a liability.

I only have myself.

And I'm helpless as long as Major has Aunt Phyllis.

She climbed up the gangway into the jet, entering a compartment just behind the cockpit. "Move aft," Major said, and silently she complied, leaving that compartment for a deluxe lounge, all creamy gold leather and rich brown wood. There were comfortable chairs, a table, a bar, a galley. "Go on," Major said. "Check out the whole thing. You'll be spending a lot of hours in here over the next few days."

Curious despite herself – she'd never been on a private jet before, never even *seen* one except in the movies – she moved through the forward lounge into the next compartment, clearly an office for Major, with a desk and luxurious chair, a computer terminal, and locked cabinets. Behind that was a bedroom, with a twin-sized bed, offset so that a corridor led past it along one side of the plane to the lavatory at the very back. She glanced into that, too: it was way roomier than the typical airline washroom. She half-expected it to boast a shower, but she supposed the water required for something like that would weigh down the plane too much and restrict its range.

Which must be pretty impressive if Major had flown across the Atlantic in this plane and now intended a direct flight from Vancouver to Honolulu, and from there to Sydney.

She made her way forward again. "It will take days to get a passport," she said to Major. "Are you going to leave poor Aunt Phyllis stuck in that little camper all that time?"

"It's not a little camper to her, it's a luxurious mansion," he said. "But not to worry. It won't take days to get a passport. I expect it to take no more than twenty-four hours."

"Don't you need all kinds of documents?" Ariane said desperately. "Proof of citizenship, photos, all kinds of stuff?"

Major just smiled. "Ordinarily, yes. But I can pull a few strings."

Ariane stared at him. "You're going to use magic to force someone to issue me a passport."

Major's smile widened. "Of course I am. What's the point of having magic if you don't use it to get what you want? Although the thing still has to get made, of course… but if you pay a $110 fee you can get twenty-four-hour urgent service. I think I can spare the $110."

"But Aunt Phyllis is still stuck in that trailer."

Major sighed. "I told you, as far as she's concerned, she's in the lap of luxury. Don't worry, she'll be well taken care of. And once you've handed over the shards to me, you and she will be free to go." The smile faded. "But never forget," he said softly, "that I can always find her again...if you cause me more trouble."

Ariane felt a surge of white-hot rage then, and *very* little of it came from the sword. But there was still nothing she could do but acquiesce, and so she turned and reentered the lounge while Major spoke to the pilot in the cabin. She couldn't hear what he was saying. A minute later he came aft. Behind him the pilot pulled up the gangway and secured the door.

"We'll be taking off right away," Major said. "It's about an hour and a half to Vancouver. We'll spend the night in a hotel. Tomorrow we'll look after your passport. With luck..." he smiled, "well, with *magic*...we'll have it by evening. We'll fly to Honolulu. I'll have to spend another day there – some of the business I need to take care of over the next couple of days doesn't lend itself to being conducted from an airplane." He made a face. "It will be a great relief when I can quit worrying about being Rex Major, businessman, and focus on being Merlin, the thousand-year-old sorcerer."

"I feel your pain," Ariane muttered.

"No one likes a sarcastic kid," Major said severely.

The engines suddenly began to whine. Major sat down opposite Ariane, and reached for the seatbelt. "Buckle up," he said. "We'll be airborne in a few minutes." He sighed. "If we don't crash on takeoff. I hate flying."

Ariane blinked at that, but reached for her own belt. "Why?"

He shuddered. "It's all based on science, not magic. I don't trust science."

The whine of the engines increased. They began to taxi, bumping across the tarmac. Ariane twisted her head and looked out the window. The Transwest Airlines turboprop that had just landed had discharged its passengers. There weren't many of them. And one of them...

She blinked.

One of them was short and slender and had bright red hair.

It can't be Wally, she thought. *He's in Toronto. It's just someone who looks like him.*

Looks a lot *like him.*

Confused, but not wanting Merlin to know what she'd seen…if she'd really seen it…she twisted her head around again. "If we crash on takeoff," she said, "what happens to the shards?"

"Someone finds them in the wreckage," Major said sourly, "and either puts them in a museum or, more likely, they end up in a landfill. The door to Faerie slams shut and magic vanishes forever from this world. So let's hope we don't crash."

I don't know, Ariane thought. *It might solve a lot of problems.*

All the same, she was glad when they made it safely into the air. As they winged their way west, she looked out the window at the clouds far below, and wondered if she had really seen what she had thought she had seen…

…and if she had, what it had meant.

CHAPTER EIGHT

KNIGHT IN SHINING ARMOUR

Wally stood on the tarmac of Glass Field, watching Rex Major's private jet dwindle into the distance. He had seen Ariane getting aboard it as they had taxied to the tiny terminal. *What is she doing with Major?* he thought, staring at that rapidly shrinking dot. *And where are they going?*

"Hey, kid, keep moving," someone yelled at him. "You can't stand there."

"Sorry!" he shouted back, and trudged on toward the terminal. He had no baggage to wait for, so he walked through the building to the front entrance, where two taxis waited. He got into the first one in line.

"Where to?" the driver asked.

"The public library," Wally said.

"Really?" the driver said. "You don't look like the studious type."

"Actually I'm looking for a computer with an Internet connection," Wally said. "I've lost my smartphone."

"Hashtag FirstWorldProblems," the driver said, and Wally groaned inwardly. Was there anything worse than a grown-up who thought he was cool?

Well, yeah, he had to admit upon reflection. *A grown-up planning to take over the world and threatening little old ladies to do so.* He forced a laugh. "I know, right? But when you gotta Snapchat, you gotta Snapchat."

"What's Snapchat?" the driver said curiously, and Wally gave up.

The John M. Cuelenaere Public Library proved to be a low-rise modern structure of tan brick with big glass windows that flooded the interior with light. He quickly located the free public Internet terminals: ten desks set up facing each other, five to a side, each with a flat-screen monitor and mouse on top and a keyboard neatly tucked away on a sliding tray underneath. There were only a couple of people using the terminals. Wally sat down in the one farthest from anyone else and slid out the keyboard. *First things first*, he thought. *Divert attention.*

The idea had come to him during the flight from Toronto. If Major hadn't heard yet about what had happened at the condo he would soon. The last thing Wally wanted him thinking was that he'd not only fled the condo, but he'd left Toronto and headed west. So a little misdirection seemed in order.

He called up his webmail home page again. There was the usual spam offering the same offers to share millions of dollars with mysterious Nigerians and cut-rate drugs to address problems he didn't expect to have for another half century or so. There was still nothing from Ariane: he hadn't really expected there would be.

He clicked the *NEW MESSAGE* button, and typed in Rex Major's address. Then he wrote: *Dear Mr. Major. So sorry for what happened. I didn't mean to hurt him. I just wanted to get out of the condo. Then I got scared and I ran. The police are probably looking for me. I'm hiding out downtown. What should I do? Help! Sorry sorry sorry. Wally.*

Not bad, he thought. He took a deep breath and clicked *Send*.

Now for my next trick...

He had spent his time on Major's computer well. He knew Major's email address and password...and how to access Major's email via the Web. Which he now did. He'd also set up a fake "Rex Major" account, but he didn't dare use it for this. Whomever "Frank" might be, he might be suspicious if he suddenly got instructions from a different account. Using Major's real account was a bit risky in its own way, but safer than the alternative. He flexed his fingers, thinking for a moment, then typed in the address he had first seen in Major's condo office: frank@ochranasecurity.com.

Frank, he typed. *Change of plans. I'm sending a taxi for our guest. There'll be a boy with it: she knows him and will go with him willingly. I've got my own people waiting for them in town. Clean up the camper and take it back. Thanks for all your good work. RM.*

He studied the email. It sounded like Rex Major in the many other emails he'd sent to Frank, and he always signed them *RM*.

Still, he hesitated. Once he sent this email, he was cutting off all ties with Major for good, even if, as he hoped, he managed to string him along a while longer. Was that really what he wanted to do? Major – Merlin – had talked such a good game, all about how he wanted to use magic to heal the ills of the world and bring an end to war and poverty and pollution and – well, you name the problem, Merlin had intimated he could solve it with magic.

But if he got that much power, Wally had always known, he would also have the power to become the worst tyrant in history. And tyrants were not known for worrying about the little people they had to crush in order to achieve their goals. Wally had convinced himself that Merlin wouldn't be like that, that the ancient wizard would be wise enough to make the world a better place without abusing the power at his command.

He'd been a fool to think it. Merlin couldn't be trusted. He'd lied to Wally...and he was using Aunt Phyllis as a hostage. Which meant he was threatening to hurt or even kill her to make Ariane do what he wanted.

I don't need any ties to a man like that, Wally thought, and sent the email.

It only took five minutes for Frank to respond. *Understood. She'll be ready. Frank.*

Wally smiled. Then he deleted the email from Major's Sent folder, and the reply from Frank from the Inbox, emptied the Deleted folder so no trace would remain – at least not in any easily accessible place – went to the front desk and phoned for a taxi.

The taxi driver, a huge man with a white beard who probably moonlighted as Santa Claus at the local mall, was more than a little suspicious when Wally told him where he wanted to go. "That quarry shut down six months ago," he growled. "Are you playing a prank?"

"No, sir," Wally said. "My...uncle is looking at taking over the quarry and he has my aunt with him. But she's not feeling well so he asked me to come get her and ride with her back to the hotel."

"Hmmph." The driver didn't sound completely convinced, but he put the car in drive and pulled away from the library. "Gonna be an expensive trip," he said over his shoulder. "Twenty minutes out and twenty minutes back plus waiting time."

Wally shrugged. "It's okay," he said. "I've got lots of money." *Lots of "Uncle Rex's" money.*

They drove out of town and in the process left behind well-paved roads for what Saskatchewan people knew as a "thin-membrane" road: a gravel road with a very thin layer of asphalt on top of it. Most of the old thin-membrane roads were being allowed to return to gravel, and this one appeared to be halfway along the process. Wally held on to the strap by his seat and tried to keep his teeth clenched so he didn't bite his tongue. The taxi driver, like every other taxi driver Wally had ever ridden with, seemed to have a sense of road-appropriate speed completely at odds with that of any normal person.

After about ten minutes of bumping through the forest, the driver turned left onto a gravel road that passed through an open gate. They trundled slowly down the rutted track between close-set trees until abruptly they emerged at the very edge of the quarry, where the road turned left and then sloped down to the snow-dusted quarry floor. "Stop here for a second," Wally said, and the driver complied. Looking out his window, Wally took in the old brown-and-cream Winnebago and the two black SUVs parked next to it. A big man in a dark suit looked up and waved. Wally took a deep breath. "Looks like they're expecting me," he said. "Let's go on down."

The driver grunted and eased the taxi down the track into the quarry. Two minutes later they rolled up to the SUVs. Wally got out. "Frank?" he said to the big man.

"Stanton," the man said. "Frank is inside helping the..." he glanced at the taxi driver, who was watching with interest. "Helping your...aunt?"

"That's right," Wally said. *This is actually going to work!* he thought, though his heart was pounding. "Aunt Phyllis. I'll go in and –"

But there was no need. The camper door opened. Another man, slightly smaller than Stanton, but not by much, and wearing an identical dark-blue suit, stepped out and then offered his arm to Aunt Phyllis. He was carrying a blue suitcase.

Aunt Phyllis looked...frazzled. Her hair stuck out in all

directions, and there was a vague, unfocused look to her face that Wally hated. But she smiled when she saw him. "Wally!" she said. "How nice! Mr. Major invited you, too!"

"That's right, Aunt Phyllis," Wally said, as Frank helped her across the uneven gravel floor of the quarry. "He's in town. He asked me to come get you and we'll go have a nice dinner together."

"Oh, that's lovely," Aunt Phyllis said warmly. She patted her frizzy hair, to no effect. "Do I look all right?"

"You look wonderful," Wally said, though his heart was breaking – breaking, and in the process releasing a level of anger that was new to him. "Let's get in the taxi." He offered his arm in turn, and Aunt Phyllis took it. She leaned harder on him than he expected. "Are you all right?" he asked her.

"Oh, couldn't be better," Aunt Phyllis said. "I've had a wonderful time. And doesn't Mr. Major have a beautiful house?" She glanced back at the old camper. "Better than any hotel."

"It's...lovely," Wally said. He glanced at Frank. "Mr. Major sends his thanks."

Frank snorted. "As long as he sends me my money, I don't need his thanks." He put the suitcase into the trunk of the taxi, then turned away. "All right, Stanton, let's close up the camper and get it out of here. Job's over."

Wally smiled to himself. He had a strong feeling Rex Major would be reneging on his final bill to Ochrana Security.

The smile faded as he looked at Aunt Phyllis, who was looking up at the clouds overhead, touched pink now by the just-setting sun, her face unworried but her mind clearly...elsewhere. *What did Major do to her?*

Voice of Command, he thought angrily. *It doesn't work on me – I don't know why. It won't work on Ariane because she has the power of the Lady. But it works on Aunt Phyllis. And I don't know how to break it.*

"Come on, Aunt Phyllis," he said gently. "You sit in the back." He opened the door for her.

"My, Wally," she said, "you're such a young gentleman." She got in and he closed the door on her, then got into the front seat with the Santa-like driver.

"Now where?" "Santa" said.

"Is there an evening bus to Saskatoon?" Wally asked.

The driver nodded. "Leaves at 6:30."

"Then the bus station, please," Wally said. He glanced at Aunt Phyllis again. He didn't know how long he had before Merlin discovered what he had done, but he did know he wanted to do his best to vanish before that happened – and the first step was to get out of Dodge.

By the time they pulled up in front of the Prince Albert bus depot, a low-rise white building with green trim, it was completely dark. Wally glanced at his watch. They still had more than hour until the bus left. He spotted a hole-in-the-wall pizza place next door. (There was also a sushi place, but he'd never really warmed up to raw fish.) *Good*, he thought. *I'm starving. And maybe eating something will snap Aunt Phyllis out of whatever spell Major's put her under.*

He didn't know why it should, but then he didn't know why it shouldn't. *I'm still new to this whole magic-is-real thing*, he thought.

He paid the driver with more of the cash he'd extracted from Major's account, and then helped Aunt Phyllis out of the taxi while the driver retrieved her suitcase. Wally took it from him while the old woman stared around. She frowned vaguely. "Where's the hotel?"

"We're going to get something to eat, Aunt Phyllis," Wally said. "This way."

The pizza place was just a short hike across the parking

lot, past the entrance to the courier/express portion of the bus depot. Wally ordered two eight-inch fully loaded pizzas and got a Diet Coke for himself and a bottle of water for Aunt Phyllis, whose frown deepened as she looked around. "Are you sure this is right, Wally?" she said faintly. "This hotel dining room…doesn't look very nice." She was staring at one wall, which featured a rather frighteningly cheerful cartoon character suspended from a red-and-yellow-striped parachute, floating down through a sky of blue tiles while carrying pizza boxes.

Wally put the drinks on the red-topped counter, and sat down next to her, placing her suitcase at his feet. "Aunt Phyllis," he said gently, "this isn't a hotel dining room. It's just a tiny pizza place."

Phyllis blinked at him. "Don't be silly, dear," she said. "Rex Major wouldn't take us to a pizza place."

"Rex Major doesn't know we're here," Wally said. "We're running away from him."

"What?" Phyllis shook her head. "No, Wally, you're wrong. Why would we run away from Mr. Major after he's been so nice to us?"

"He's not just Mr. Major, remember, Aunt Phyllis?" Wally said. "He's really Merlin. He's a sorcerer. And he's put some kind of spell on you." He looked at the workers in the kitchen, and a woman with a small child in tow who had just come in and was ordering at the counter, and lowered his voice. "Aunt Phyllis. He wants the shards of Excalibur. Ariane is trying to get to them first. The Lady of the Lake gave us a quest. We went to the Northwest Territories and to France to try to stop him. Remember?"

"But that was just a big misunderstanding," Aunt Phyllis said. "Mr. Major explained it to me. It was just… " Her voice faltered. "…a… " She frowned. "…a…game?" Her expression cleared. "Yes, that's it. It was just a game.

A reality show. *Like The Greatest Race.* And Mr. Major won, and then you went to visit him in Toronto, but he came to visit me at Emma Lake, and then he invited me to his place in Prince Albert, and I was having a lovely time but then you showed up and brought me here." Suddenly her eyes widened. "Wally! Did you lie when you said Mr. Major wanted me to come with you?"

"No," Wally said hastily. "No, Aunt Phyllis. Mr. Major sent an email to Frank at his...house...and told him I would be coming by taxi to pick you up. Frank would never have let you go with me if Mr. Major hadn't told him it was all right, would he?"

"No...no, I suppose not." But Aunt Phyllis, staring at the parachuting-pizza-deliveryman cartoon again, still looked confused. "But this hotel..."

"The hotel we're meeting Rex Major at isn't in Prince Albert, it's in Saskatoon," Wally said. If he were somehow going to free Aunt Phyllis from Rex Major's powerful Command, a pizza place in P.A. clearly wasn't the best place to attempt it. "We're going to take the bus to Saskatoon, and we'll join him there."

"Oh," Aunt Phyllis said. "Well, that's all right then."

The pizzas arrived. Aunt Phyllis ate hers with evident relish, but Wally, to his surprise, found he wasn't nearly as hungry as he had been.

He'd hoped, once he had Aunt Phyllis free of Major's men, that she'd snap back to normal. But now he was wondering if anyone *could* bring her back to normal except Merlin. And if that were the case...then Aunt Phyllis *still* wasn't free – and Merlin *still* had a hostage to force Ariane to do what he wanted.

He still has a hostage as long as Ariane doesn't know she's free, too, Wally reminded himself. *I have to get word to her somehow. But I don't even know where they're going.*

Unless…

"Aunt Phyllis," he said cautiously.

"Yes, dear?" Aunt Phyllis said, after swallowing her last bite of pizza and wiping her mouth delicately with her napkin.

"Have you seen Ariane recently?"

"Of course, dear," Aunt Phyllis said. "She came to visit me at Mr. Major's house." She frowned. "Although I only talked to her for a moment. I dozed off."

"Did she or Mr. Major mention…anywhere in particular?"

"I don't know what you mean, Wally."

"I mean…going somewhere. Like…planning a trip."

"I'm afraid I slept through it if they did," Aunt Phyllis said apologetically. "The only people I heard talking about a trip were Frank and Stanton."

"Yeah?" Wally said. He leaned forward. "Where were they planning to go?"

"Oh, I don't think they were planning to go," Aunt Phyllis said. "They just said they'd like to go, and something about 'lucky brat.' Rather rude of them, but I don't know who they were talking about."

Ariane, Wally thought, heart leaping. "Where did they say they wanted to go?"

"Australia," Aunt Phyllis said. "By private jet." She laughed. "As if anyone could just hop in a private jet and fly to Australia!"

Australia, Wally thought. *They've gone to Australia.*

And then, *I need a computer.*

Wally prided himself on knowing his way around the Internet…and one site he had stumbled on months ago allowed anyone to track any flight, private or public – as long as you knew the number on the plane's tail.

Which he did. He'd taken note of the number on Major's jet as it had taken off from Prince Albert. He could track the flight, find out exactly where they were going: make his own arrangements, and hopefully get wherever they were going not too far behind them. And then...what?

Find them, if I can. Follow them, I guess. Try to get a message to Ariane.

But if Aunt Phyllis remained in thrall to Merlin it wouldn't change anything. To get Major to break the spell, she'd *still* have to do what Major wanted, and hand over the third shard of Excalibur as soon as they found it.

It's a two-hour bus ride to Saskatoon, he thought. *Maybe Aunt Phyllis will snap out of it.*

And if she doesn't?

He shoved the thought away and concentrated on the last of his pizza. It looked delicious – but to Wally, it now tasted like sawdust. He'd been ecstatic after successfully rescuing Aunt Phyllis, but now he was beginning to realize it might only be the beginning of his struggle to redeem himself – and help Ariane complete the quest they had both been given.

I still don't know if we can trust the Lady, Wally thought, *but I'm* damn *sure we can't trust Rex Major.*

Too bad it had taken his complete betrayal of his best friend for him to find that out.

Pizza eaten, they crossed the parking lot again and went into the bus depot, where Wally purchased two one-way tickets to Saskatoon.

They'd need a place to stay in Saskatoon, and he preferred to have it lined up before they left Prince Albert rather than leave it to chance. The Prince Albert bus depot didn't offer terminals for public use, unlike Pearson International Airport. He snorted. *Go figure.* He'd have to book a hotel over the phone. He'd need a credit card for that, and he didn't have one. But Aunt Phyllis...

He went over to where she sat quietly, staring off at

nothing. "Aunt Phyllis," he said.

"Where is Mr. Major?" she said, sounding peevish. "I'm getting quite tired and would like him to show us to our rooms."

"We're meeting him in Saskatoon, Aunt Phyllis, remember?" Wally said.

She frowned. "Saskatoon?" She shook her head. "No, I don't think that's right. Can you take me home, please? Maybe Mr. Major is waiting for us there."

Wally felt a rising tide of frustration. "He's meeting us in Saskatoon, Aunt Phyllis," he said, an edge to his voice that he felt bad about but couldn't control. "We're taking the bus."

"The bus?" Aunt Phyllis shook her head, and to Wally's horror, stood up. She brushed the front of her skirt. "No, Wally, I'm sorry, but I'm not going with you on the bus. I'm taking a taxi back to Rex Major's lovely home. You've clearly made a mistake. Rex Major would –"

"Aunt Phyllis, stop it!" Wally said, frustration boiling over into full-blown anger and annoyance. "Snap out of it!"

The phrase came out like a command, a crackling snap of sound that turned heads in their direction.

And then Aunt Phyllis, with a soft moan, sank down into her chair and slumped to one side, unconscious.

CHAPTER NINE

THE VISION

ARIANE SPENT THE FLIGHT to Vancouver very deliberately not talking to Rex Major. He didn't seem to care. He retired to the office space aft of the main cabin as soon as they were airborne and didn't emerge for the rest of the flight.

Exploring, Ariane found cheese and crackers and pop and bottled water and wine and a few more exotic liqueurs in tiny airline bottles in the galley, though there didn't seem to be any actual meals. She made herself a snack plate and grabbed a bottle of water. She'd tasted wine and hadn't liked it and didn't think this was a good day to start drinking whisky, even if Major was unlikely to object to the fact she was underage...although for a minute she was tempted. She'd heard getting drunk made you forget things, and forgetting what was happening to her sounded tempting.

But she drank her water instead, and ate her cheddar and rice crackers, and hoped Aunt Phyllis was all right, and tried to think of a plan for stealing the shard Major had given her, using her magic to get back to Prince Albert, and...

...somehow getting past the armed guards at Aunt Phyllis's door when there was no water anywhere near, except for whatever little she could draw from the storage tanks on the Winnebago itself, which hardly seemed likely to be sufficient.

As promised, the flight was an hour and a half, and by the end of it, she was no closer to finding a solution than when they had started.

When the pilot announced they'd started their final descent into Vancouver, Rex Major emerged from his office. "I've booked hotel rooms in Vancouver. But if you're thinking of making a run for it, just remember..."

"...you have Aunt Phyllis. I'm not likely to forget," Ariane said sourly.

"Good," Major said.

His cell phone chirped. He glanced at it and frowned. "I'll deal with it when we're down," he said, as if to himself, and reached for the seat belts built into the bench seating along the walls. "Buckle up," he said. "It could be a bumpy descent."

She remembered that he hated flying and gave him an unsympathetic smile. "Doesn't bother me," she said sweetly. It was a very minor bit of payback, but it made her feel better.

She fastened her own belt and stared past Major at the windows behind him. They'd stayed ahead of the sunset and had been flying through bright blue skies, but now there was nothing to be seen outside but thick grey cloud – cloud that didn't clear until they were so close to the ground it took Ariane by surprise when it appeared. Three minutes later they touched down in a driving rain, and rolled across the shining wet pavement to a hangar bearing the Excalibur Computer Systems logo. The pilot taxied into its cavernous interior, then shut down the engines.

"Here we are," Major said. But his eyes had gone back to the cell phone. "Stay put," he said. "I need to follow up on this." He got up and went into his office, and closed the door.

Ariane stared at the closed door. Then she glanced at the door into the cockpit as it opened. The pilot gave her a noncommittal look, and went down the stairs.

All alone, Ariane thought. *Well, then...*

She crept to the office door and pressed her head against it.

It was more soundproof than she would have liked, but she could catch a few intelligible phrases. In fact, they leaped out at her. "Wally...somewhere downtown...hiding from police...find him...all right. Keep me posted."

She hurried back to her seat and tried to look as if she'd been there all the time. The door opened. Major jerked his head toward the front of the cabin. "Let's go," he said shortly. "A car is waiting."

She followed him, but all she was thinking about was what she had just heard. Wally hiding in downtown Toronto...from the police? What could have happened? *If he's in Toronto, that couldn't have been him I saw in Prince Albert...*

Why do you even care? another part of her whispered. *He betrayed you.*

That's right, she told herself. *I don't* care what happens *to him anymore. He can drop* dead *for all I care.*

But as she followed Major down the jet's stairs onto the floor of the hangar, then across the concrete to the exit, another thought lodged itself in her brain and refused to go away.

I hope he's all right.

◀▶

Rex Major fumed as he led Ariane out of the hangar to the big black limousine waiting outside. *Insolent brat*, he thought. *I told him to stay put. Who does he think he is?*

He's immune to Command, for one thing, he reminded himself. *And that's because he may well be heir to Arthur's power.*

His black mood lifted a little. In fact, he was *certain* Wally was heir to Arthur's power now. He'd read Iftekhar's report on what had happened...what he remembered of it. Apparently the boy had shown astonishing martial ability, using the poker like a sword to overcome a man twice his size, twice his age, and with years of training.

As more and more of Excalibur is uncovered, Major thought, *its power is making itself felt everywhere. It's a conduit for magic from Faerie. Every piece of it draws more power through the doorway from home.* He rubbed the ruby stud in his earlobe. *Even I'm feeling it. The Commands I gave Phyllis...before the first two shards were discovered, I could never have taken control of her mind so thoroughly.*

It was one reason he was confident he could expedite the replacement of Ariane's passport. A Command in the right ear, and the fact he wasn't her legal guardian, the fact he had no proof of her citizenship with him, and assorted other difficulties would simply vanish into thin air.

On the Passport Canada website, prominently labelled "Fraud alert!", was the statement that "No third-party person or group can speed up the processing of your passport application." *Want to bet?* Major thought.

The boy had panicked. Understandable. He had no idea what power he was heir to. And apparently he'd messed up Iftekhar's head pretty good. Scalp wounds bled a lot. He'd probably thought he'd murdered the man instead of just stunning him.

He's probably lucky he didn't, Major thought. *If the*

sword really is feeding power to him, the kind of power Arthur had...

I'll have to handle him more gently going forward. Don't want him accidentally killing a guard. I can cover up a lot, but that would be difficult.

First things first. Reassure Wally and get him to go back to the condo. He opened the door of the limousine and slid onto the smooth white leather of its back seat. Ariane slid in beside him and silently fastened her seatbelt. He clicked his own into place. "Let's go," he said to the driver. The car rolled away from the hangar.

It was a short trip. Merlin had booked at the Fairmont Vancouver Airport, a luxury hotel located directly above the international terminal. Five minutes after they left the Excalibur Computer Systems hangar they were pulling up to the entrance. Five minutes after that, Ariane was safely ensconced in a luxurious room on the hotel's fourteenth floor, with a spectacular view of the North Shore mountains and the airport's landing runways. Major showed her how to use the touch-screen system that adjusted the in-room environmental controls, and for a moment she seemed to forget he was her enemy, as she exclaimed with delight. He rather enjoyed her enjoyment of the room. He sometimes forgot, living the lifestyle he did, that not everyone else did.

Then he opened the adjoining door to his room, and re-established their proper relationship. "Don't think you can sneak away without me being aware of it," he warned her.

"You going to come in and watch me shower?" she snapped. "Is that how you get your kicks? Even if you did I could vanish before you could do anything about it."

Major shoved down a surge of anger. *More insolence. She and Wally deserve each other. Too bad I stole him away from her.* "I don't need to," he said evenly. "The minute you leave, I call the people watching Aunt Phyllis."

He pointed her to her room. "But this door stays open."

Ariane folded her arms. "I don't have anything with me. I need toothpaste and a toothbrush and other things, too. Girl things."

Major groaned. "Call room service. They can send up whatever you need." He pointed at the other room again. "Now get in there and leave me alone."

"I didn't ask to be abducted," Ariane said, but left him alone, vanishing out of sight around the corner.

Unlike Ariane, Major had an overnight bag with him and, of course, his computer. He opened it and connected to the WiFi network. He checked his inbox, watching the email pouring in as the computer found the Excalibur Computer Systems server. Lots to work through. It would take him a while.

He went to the minibar, pulled out a small whisky bottle, emptied its contents into a glass, and set to work.

◄◄ ►►

Ariane took a shower. The hotel provided big fuzzy bathrobes, and she made certain hers was well-belted before she left the bathroom and passed in front of the open door to Major's room. But he was out of sight, presumably at the desk.

It was too early to go to bed, but she didn't want to put her clothes back on now that the rest of her was clean. As she'd discovered long since, ordering the water off of them did nothing to take away the gunk the water had deposited, and since her recent activity had all been in shallow Saskatchewan lakes, there'd been lots of gunk to deposit.

Then again...this was a hotel. A fancy one. She looked at the guest services brochure. Sure enough, they offered laundry service. And the other things she needed. Plus, she was hungry.

She made a call. She stuffed her clothes into a plastic bag she found in the closet. Then she turned on the TV and channel-surfed while she waited.

About ten minutes later there was a knock at the door. "Room service," said a voice.

"Who is it?" Major called at once. He appeared in the doorway. She pulled the bathrobe even tighter.

"Room service," she repeated. "You said..."

Major frowned and went to the door. "Yes?" he snapped as he opened it.

"Um...room service?" said the young man on the other side. He had a trolley. "Some toiletries and, uh," he checked a piece of paper in his hand, "a Caesar salad, fish and chips, and warm apple pie? Plus a Diet Coke?"

Major looked at Ariane.

"You said," she repeated, "'Call room service, and they can bring up anything you need.'"

He sighed. "Yes, I did. Well, it will hardly break me." He stepped aside. "Bring it in."

The young man came in. He looked at Ariane, looked at Major, didn't *quite* raise an eyebrow, and held out the chit to be signed. Major signed it and handed it back. "Now get out," he said.

"Not yet," Ariane said. She got up from the bed and handed the young man the plastic bag with her clothes in it. "They told me you normally provide laundry services only if you have the clothes in by 9 a.m. but I thought if maybe I asked really nicely...I really need them by morning." She gave him a bright smile.

"I'll see to it," he said, smiling back. He turned and rolled the trolley back into the hallway.

"Thank you!" Ariane called as he turned to close the door. He gave her a wink and then the door snicked shut.

"You flirted with him," Major said. "To get him to help you."

"We can't all just order people to do what we want them to do," Ariane said. "I've got to work with what I've got."

Major grunted. "Enjoy your meal," he said, and went into the other room.

By the time she'd eaten, Ariane was exhausted. She'd used her power a lot the previous day, then had a short and sleepless night. Throw in the shock of Aunt Phyllis's abduction, the car ride and the plane flight, and she had nothing left. She turned off the light and got into bed, only slipping off the bathrobe once the covers were up to her chin, and making sure she could reach it in an emergency.

Major's light stayed on, and she could hear the tap-tap-tap of his keyboard. But not for long, because almost at once she fell asleep.

She dreamed.

When she had first begun to feel the Lady's power working through her, she had often dreamed of lakes and swords, echoes of the ancient world of Excalibur's youth. But those dreams had vanished with the Lady's departure.

Then there had been the frightening dreams, haunted by the demon Merlin had summoned to try to keep her from sleeping, to wear her down so she could not find the second shard before he did. She had banished that demon with the power of the first shard.

Since then, she had had only ordinary dreams...until now.

She recognized at once that this was one of those *other* kinds of dreams, a vivid image painted in her mind by magic. Once again there was a lake...but this was no shallow Saskatchewan pond, or even the deeper and colder northern lake where her aunt's cabin was. This was a lake she had never seen before, a striking blue colour, surrounded by thinly forested slopes rising to snow-capped mountain peaks to which clung wisps of cloud.

There was a small, rocky island close to one shore. In her dream she crossed the water, though not by boat: she seemed to have no body in the dream, just as she had no body when she traversed the world in the clouds. Then she was on the island. She slipped, somehow, through a small opening between two rocks. Inside was a pool, deep and still. And in the bottom of the pool...

The song of the sword pierced her mind, hard and cold and wild and filled with longing, the longing to be reunited with the other shards already freed from their ancient hiding places.

The third shard. The one she was looking for. The one they were flying to Australia to find. It was in *that* pool, on *that* island, in *that* lake.

The dream...the vision...began to fade. But she had the power to choose to focus on any part of the world of the vision. She used that power to streak back across the water. There was a small gravel parking lot, and a sign, green with yellow letters:

Lake Putahi. Elevation 720 m.

The song of the sword crescendoed. She found herself screaming back. "I'm coming! I'm coming! I'm..."

She snapped awake, gasping, heart pounding.

"What have you seen?" said a voice by her bed, and she jerked her head to the right and clutched at the covers. Major stood there in his own white bathrobe. "You've had a vision, haven't you?" he said intently. "Of the third shard."

She nodded.

"Tell me."

"It...it's in a pool," she said, pulse still racing. "On an island. In a lake. Surrounded by mountains. Tall ones, with snow."

"Rugged mountains? As rugged as the Rockies?"

"Maybe even more rugged," she said. "And I saw a

name. On a sign, in the parking lot. 'Lake Putahi.'"

"Maori," Major said at once. "And that means the shard isn't in Australia at all. Most likely it's in New Zealand. Get up. We'll see what Google makes of it."

"I'm not getting up until you leave the room," Ariane said.

He sighed. "Fine." He turned and went out.

Ariane grabbed her bathrobe and put it on under the covers, then slipped out of her bed and padded barefoot into Major's room. He was already seated at his computer. "It *is* New Zealand," he said. "South Island. The Lakes District of the Southern Alps. Look."

He turned the screen toward her and she saw a photograph of the same lake she had seen in her dreams a moment before. "The name means, roughly, 'Cloud Lake.' Or maybe 'The Lake in the Clouds.'" He typed some more. "It's an hour or so from Queenstown... which has an airport we can land at. Perfect." He turned the computer back toward himself. "Go back to bed," he said without looking at her. "I'll contact the pilot."

Ariane stared at him for a moment, then returned to her room. She tugged off the bathrobe and slipped back under the covers. *New Zealand.* All she knew about New Zealand was that *The Hobbit* and *The Lord of the Rings* movies had been shot there. And something about kiwi. *Is that a fruit or a bird?* She couldn't remember.

I can't believe I'm going to New Zealand, she thought; and then, *I can't believe I just told Rex Major exactly where the third shard of Excalibur is.*

But as long as he had Aunt Phyllis, what else could she do?

It still felt like betrayal. Only this time, instead of being betrayed by someone else, she was the one doing the betraying. Betraying the Lady. Betraying herself. Even betraying the sword Excalibur, which had reached out to her to tell her where the third part of it was.

I'm doing what I think is right, she thought.

So was Wally, a small voice murmured.

That unsettling thought followed her down to sleep.

CHAPTER TEN

THE BUS AND THE BANK

I'VE KILLED HER! WALLY THOUGHT, staring down at Aunt Phyllis in horror. Heads were beginning to turn all around the bus depot. A security guard took a step toward them.

But then, to his immense relief, Aunt Phyllis blinked, straightened, and looked around her. "Where...where am I?" she said. She glanced up. "Wally? Is that you?"

"Of course it is, Aunt Phyllis." Wally gave the guard what he hoped was a bright reassuring grin, though he suspected it had a slightly frantic look to it. He gave up, wiped it away, and sat down next to Aunt Phyllis. "Don't you remember? I came and got you in a taxi...?"

"From the cabin?" Aunt Phyllis said faintly. Then she frowned. "No...I was somewhere else..." She put a hand to her head. "It's all so confusing," she said. "Did I have a stroke?"

"No!" Wally hastened to reassure her, putting his hand on hers and giving it a squeeze. "Nothing like that. You've been..." *This is going to sound weird*, he thought, but he couldn't lie to her. "...under a spell."

She blinked. "A spell?" And then her eyes widened. "Rex Major. He came to the cottage. He..." She blinked again. "What did he do to me?"

"He used magic on you," Wally said. "This thing he does, called the Voice of Command. He can tell people what to do, and they have to do it. And he told you to believe that you were visiting him in a very nice house, and that he was your friend, and everything was all right. But really you were in an old camper in an abandoned quarry, being held prisoner."

Aunt Phyllis shook her head. "I can almost see it..." she said. "I can see the house I thought I was in, but that's fading, like something from a dream. A camper... two men..." And then her eyes flew wide again. "Ariane! Ariane was there! What –"

"Major was holding you hostage," Wally said. "He was holding you hostage to force Ariane to help him. They've gone in search of the third shard."

"Gone? Gone where?" Aunt Phyllis said.

"Australia, I think," Wally said. "I've got to find out."

"And where are we now?" Aunt Phyllis stared around. "Oh! I know this place. It's the Prince Albert bus station."

"That's right," Wally said, and the mere fact she knew that made him feel much happier. "We're heading to Saskatoon to start with."

Aunt Phyllis looked at him with something like the usual twinkle in her eye. "To start with? Does this mean we're on the lam?"

Wally blinked. "The lam?"

Aunt Phyllis sighed. "On the run. Don't you ever watch old movies?"

"Sure. I've watched the original *Star Wars* twenty times."

Aunt Phyllis laughed. "Never mind."

The announcement came over the public address system that the bus for Saskatoon was loading. Aunt Phyllis got up. "We'll talk more on the bus," she said. "You can tell me exactly what that man did to me...and what's happening with Ariane. And then you do whatever you have to to help her. You hear me, young man?"

"Yes," Wally said meekly. "I hear you."

Feeling immensely relieved, he followed Aunt Phyllis to the bus, put her suitcase down to be loaded into the cargo area, and showed the tickets. He realized as he followed her aboard that he still hadn't made a hotel reservation for them in Saskatoon. *Hopefully there's not a big convention on and we won't have any trouble finding a place,* he thought.

They sat about halfway back, where the sound of the bus would drown out their voices. As they rolled out of town and down the highway for the hour-and-a-half journey, Wally told Aunt Phyllis everything that had happened – including how he had come to betray Ariane in France, and why.

She listened silently to that part, then put her hand on his. "I understand, Wally," she said, and for some reason his eyes suddenly felt hot and wet. "You care about Ariane, more than you care about this insane quest the...Lady of the Lake" – Wally had the distinct impression she'd intended to add a probably *colourful* adjective before the Lady's name and had thought better of it – "set you on. And Rex Major can be very persuasive..."

"But he didn't Command me," Wally said miserably. "I'm immune to it. I don't know why."

"He can be persuasive *without* magic," Aunt Phyllis said. "Or he wouldn't be as good a businessman as he clearly is. He told you just enough truth to make you think that *everything* he said was the truth, so that when he switched to lies, you'd still believe him. He played on your biggest weakness: your feelings for Ariane."

"She's not my girlfriend," Wally said automatically. *And probably never will be now.*

"I didn't say she was," Aunt Phyllis said. "But she's still your friend, and what he told you about the sword changing her is clearly the truth. She *did* hurt your sister. She hurt *you*, getting the second shard. I don't think she meant to do either one, but the power she has...how could it *not* be changing her?"

"I think it's changing me, too," Wally said. "Whatever this...secret...about me is that Rex Major wouldn't tell me, it's connected to the sword. And there have been... weird things happening. And not just my being able to break you free from Merlin's spell just now."

He told her what Ariane had told him about the two shards singing in perfect harmony when he held them, but singing discordantly when she held them, so that she could not use them together. He told her about his sudden surge of fencing skill, which had so impressed Coach Mueller she'd intended to send him to the big Chinook Open fencing competition in Swift Current. And then he told her what he'd done to the guard outside Rex Major's condo. "I may have killed him," he said. "I hope I didn't, but I may have. And I did it without thinking...just the way Ariane hurt Flish. It's got to be the sword's influence. But why is it affecting *me*?"

Aunt Phyllis shook her head. "I don't know, Wally. But I don't see any way to stop it. You've just got to push ahead...you and Ariane...and get the shards of Excalibur before Merlin can."

"I know," Wally said. He sighed. "Ariane has the first one. Merlin has the second one. And Ariane thinks he still has you hostage. She'll find the third one for him and give him the first two unless I can somehow reach her, tell her you're free. If I don't...his power must be growing, too. Look what he did to you! With all three shards in his hands, we won't stand a chance."

"What will you do?"

"If they're heading to Australia, I need to get there, too," Wally said.

Aunt Phyllis sighed. "I helped you get to France, but I can't pay for a trip to Australia, Wally."

Wally smiled then. "You won't have to," he said. "As long as we get to a bank machine in time, Rex Major will."

"Really?" Aunt Phyllis laughed. "I'm not sure how you're going to make that happen, but I heartily approve."

"The bigger problem will be figuring out exactly where they go," Wally said. "Australia is a big place. But if I can get to a computer, I can at least figure out which airport they're flying to. After that..." He sighed. "I guess I wing it."

"You've done pretty good so far, Wally," Aunt Phyllis said, patting his hand again. "I have every confidence in you."

Well, that makes one of us, Wally thought, and settled back in his seat. He stared out the window into the darkness. *I wonder where Ariane is right now?*

◄◄ ►►

There was a Hilton Garden Inn within a block of the Saskatoon bus depot. After arriving, Wally and Aunt Phyllis walked across the street into the big parking lot that served both the hotel and the Midtown Plaza shopping mall, Wally carrying the suitcase, and made their way to the hotel's lobby. "Do you have a reservation?" the pretty, brown-skinned young woman behind the counter said in a pronounced East Indian accent.

"No," Aunt Phyllis said. They'd decided it would be less suspicious if the grown-up did the talking. "We didn't know we were coming until today. Do you have any rooms?"

"Well, we've been pretty full, but you're in luck," the

woman said, checking her computer. "We've had a cancellation. If you don't mind sharing...?"

Okay, that's awkward, Wally thought, but Aunt Phyllis simply said, "That will be fine." She handed over her credit card. Wally hoped she'd managed to pay off enough of the France trip that it would still cover the hotel room. Apparently it did; a few moments later they were riding the elevator to the sixth floor.

The room was nice enough, with two double beds. Wally said, "Before we do anything else, I need to get to a bank machine to make that transfer we talked about. There's a Royal Bank not far from here..."

Aunt Phyllis nodded. She opened her big black purse and pulled out a green fake-alligator-skin wallet. She held out her bank card. "You remember the PIN number?"

"7556?" The last four digits of Aunt Phyllis's phone number. Not the most secure choice, but he didn't say anything about it. His own PIN number was 1701, from NCC-1701, the registry number of the *U.S.S. Enterprise* in the original *Star Trek* series. Although come to think of it, anyone who knew him well might be able to figure that out. *Logically, I should probably change it*, he thought, and grinned to himself.

"Will this really work?" Aunt Phyllis said.

"If Rex Major hasn't caught on yet that I've drained most of his personal account, then it should," Wally said. "I left enough so he shouldn't run short making ordinary purchases, and I would think he's been a little too busy to check his banking statement, so I think there's a real good chance."

"Well, be careful."

"I will," Wally promised, though he wondered what he was supposed to be careful about. Admittedly it was dark, and downtown Saskatoon could be a little sketchy, but it was still early evening. And Major clearly still hadn't caught up to what was going on, or – as Wally had secretly feared would be the case, though he'd said nothing to Aunt Phyllis about it – there would have been hired goons in a big black car waiting for them when they came out of the bus depot.

At least she cares, he thought as he took the elevator back down to the lobby. *That's more than my own parents do.*

Thinking of his parents made him wonder how Flish was doing, and he felt a pang of guilt as he realized that he hadn't called her again since that one uncomfortable conversation after he'd come home from France.

She's never going to forgive me, either.

He crossed 22nd Street, then 1st Avenue. The Royal Bank was on the corner of 1st and 23rd, directly across from the main entrance to the Midtown Plaza. He went to the ATMs. The first thing he did was check the balance in his account. If Major had somehow managed to reverse the transaction, then…

But, no, the balance in his account was larger than it had been in his entire life. It didn't come close to the total in his trust fund, of course, but he couldn't touch that for another seven years. It was certainly more than enough to get him wherever he needed to go.

He dug into his backpack and took out the cheque.

He'd made plans for this before he'd left Major's condo. In fact it had been far easier than he'd anticipated. He'd thought he'd have to somehow get to a bank and get a supply of emergency cheques, but when he'd been poking around on Major's computer he'd discovered the computer magnate printed his own cheques as needed. A tweaking of the software to put his account number, name and address on the cheques instead of Rex Major's, and he'd been able to print out fifty of them with no trouble at all.

Cheques, he'd reasoned, would be harder to track than online transactions of any kind. *As long as they actually go through.* He looked down at the cheque. He'd had to Google to find out how to fill it out: he'd never written a cheque in his life.

The cheque was made out to Phyllis Forsythe, for $50,000.

He removed his card from the machine, inserted hers, put in her pin number, chose *Deposit*, followed the instructions, inserted the envelope.

The machine accepted it.

He was limited in how much money he could transfer from the account into which he had just deposited the $50,000, but he paid off as much of her credit card bill as he could. The rest might take most of a day – and might not transfer at all if Rex Major twigged to what was going on.

Better spend it before he does, Wally thought.

Walking back to the hotel, Wally was uneasily aware he still wasn't being completely honest with Aunt Phyllis. There was one thing he'd discovered on Major's computer he still hadn't shared with her: the blurry security-cam photograph of her sister. He wondered if he should tell her. There was nothing she could do about it and she might be hurt to think that her sister hadn't even been in touch since her disappearance, while she struggled with illness and then the challenges of looking after Ariane...

He caught himself in mid-thought. Who was he to withhold information like that from Aunt Phyllis? Who was he to decide what was good for her and what wasn't? It was the same mistake he'd made with Ariane. He'd tried to protect her and only made things worse. If he'd just trusted her and acted like her friend instead of trying to protect her as if he were her father (or boyfriend, but he shied away from that thought almost as soon as it formed), they would have had both shards and gone on to find the third. He'd let Major convince him that the shards were changing Ariane in dangerous ways. But now he'd discovered the shards were changing *him* in dangerous ways, too, and he'd also discovered it didn't matter. There was no going back. And there was certainly no giving in to Major, who had revealed his true colours by kidnapping Aunt Phyllis, holding her hostage, and threatening to hurt her if Ariane didn't do exactly what he wanted her to do.

All five shards of Excalibur would be discovered. Clearly there was no way to prevent it. That meant the only question was who would have the sword in the end – Ariane (and the Lady of the Lake), or Merlin. And now that Merlin had belied all the fine words he'd plied Wally with, there was clearly only one answer to that question.

Just as there was clearly only one answer to the question, *Should I tell Aunt Phyllis about her sister or not?*

So when he got back to the hotel, the first thing he did was go to the business centre, access his email, and print the photo of Emily Forsythe he had found on Major's computer and forwarded to himself. Then he rode the elevator back up to the room. He had other things he needed to do on the hotel computers, but this came first.

"Did it work?" Aunt Phyllis asked as he came in.

"Yes," he said. "I couldn't transfer all of it because the cheque has to go through whatever mystical process banks put cheques through, but I paid off a couple of thousand dollars of your credit card. Which should give you enough credit to get me to…wherever I have to go. I still need to figure that out. But, Aunt Phyllis…there's something else I need to tell you first."

Aunt Phyllis was sitting, in nightgown and robe, in the armchair by the window. "What is it, dear?"

Wally pulled the office chair out from behind the desk and turned it around so he could sit facing her. "I found this on Rex Major's computer." He held out the photo he had just printed.

Aunt Phyllis took it, looked at it. For a moment she didn't seem to understand what she was seeing…then her eyes widened. "Oh…" she said softly. "Oh." And then her eyes filled with tears.

Feeling awkward, but also feeling that he couldn't just sit there, Wally got up from the office chair and squeezed next to her on the armchair and put his arms around her. She leaned into him. "Oh, Wally," she said softly. "I was so sure she was dead. I thought I was over it. I thought… how can she be alive? Why hasn't she contacted us?'

Wally had no answer to that. "I don't know," he said. "I think she must be very afraid."

"Of Rex Major," Aunt Phyllis said, and it wasn't a question.

"Of Rex Major," Wally agreed, but wondered how much of her fear was of Major, and how much was of the Lady of the Lake. The Lady had approached Emily Forsythe first, tried to get her to take her power, and she had refused it. Ariane had not. Who had made the right choice?

She doesn't even know about Ariane, Wally thought then. *She doesn't know her daughter accepted the power she refused. She left to try to protect Ariane, and it didn't work out any better than when I betrayed Ariane to try to protect her.*

And even the attempt to escape Major was in peril of failing. Major had a lead. He knew where she'd been, on a specific date. And he had the resources to track her down. How far along her trail was he? Would Major take Ariane's mother hostage next?

And if he does, Wally thought uneasily, *there won't be anyone in the right place at the right time to find out where she is and rescue her the way I rescued Aunt Phyllis. If*

Major finds her, Ariane will give up every shard she has and help him find all the others to save her mother – no matter how the power of the sword fights against that urge.

Which means...

He sighed. *Which means, once we've sorted out the third shard, we have to start looking for Ariane's mother ourselves. We need to find her first.*

The cliché: *it never rains but it pours* came to mind. Wasn't one quest enough? Now they'd have to deal with two.

Not unless we keep that third shard from Major, he reminded himself. *First things first.*

He squeezed Aunt Phyllis's shoulder. "We'll find her," he said. "We'll find her before he does. We have to."

Aunt Phyllis nodded silently.

Wally eased himself away from her and stood up. "I need to go back down to the business centre," he said. "Will you be all right?"

Aunt Phyllis reached for a tissue from the box on the table by the chair and blew her nose. "I'll be fine," she said with a wan smile. But when Wally went to the door and glanced back, he saw her reaching for another tissue, as she sat in the chair staring at the picture he had given her.

He closed the door quietly and went to the elevator.

I'm only fourteen years old, Wally thought as he rode down to the lobby once again. *How did I end up being the one in charge?*

There was no answer to that except that someone had to be, if Rex Major was going to be stopped.

In the business centre, Wally sat down and called up the flight-tracking website he'd discovered. He typed in the tail number of Major's private jet, and...

There it was. The plane had flown to Vancouver. It currently showed no new flight plan. Wally frowned. Flight plans could show up anywhere from twenty-four hours to thirty minutes before the flight took place. If Rex Major were planning to fly to Australia for certain, he'd have expected the pilot to have already filed the flight plan. But he hadn't.

Did that mean Major didn't know for sure where he was going next?

And if that was the case, why had he flown first to Vancouver?

He thought about it, hard. *He's planning to fly to Australia...or at least somewhere down there. Another country. He has Ariane with her. And Ariane...*

Ah.

Ariane doesn't have a passport. She lost it in the cave in France.

Which meant Major was stuck in Canada until he could get her one, and even the most urgent request could only get a passport within about twenty-four hours. Wally had another day, at least.

What he really hoped was that Major's pilot would file a flight plan as soon as his boss told him where they were going. In which case, there was a fighting chance he could actually get to wherever Major was taking Ariane *before* they did.

But until the pilot filed his flight plan, there was nothing he could do.

He yawned. *Except sleep.*

Which, suddenly, seemed more important than anything else.

He pushed away from the computer desk and headed to the elevator. He was leaving the elevator, thinking about the photo he'd left Aunt Phyllis staring at, when a horrible thought struck him with so much force he stopped dead in the hallway, feeling sick.

The photo had been taken from a security camera. Merlin's magic wove through computer networks worldwide.

Clearly he had been monitoring security cameras for people of interest, or he never would have gotten that photo of Ariane's mother.

Wally didn't think his magic was in *every* network – not every network used Excalibur Computer Systems software. But enough did that you could never be sure.

He had just used an ATM. And ATMs had security cameras.

Was an alarm even now going off on Rex Major's computer – or in his head, through magic?

Rex Major had operatives in Saskatoon. There would be a branch of Ochrana Security for sure, and even failing that, there was his own staff. In Regina he'd Commanded his district sales manager to try to kidnap Ariane. If he discovered through the security camera that Wally was in Saskatoon, he would send someone to try to find him – no question. He might dig deeper into other computer networks he had access to. And that might lead them right to the hotel.

For a second Wally thought he'd have to tell Aunt Phyllis to get dressed, tell her they were leaving the hotel for somewhere else…but he couldn't do that. Not after the day she'd had. *He won't send people into the hotel to roust us out*, he thought. *He'll have them waiting for us when we leave. If he even figures out where we are.*

They'd have to leave early in the morning, get out of the hotel through a back exit, find somewhere to hide Aunt Phyllis that was safe from Major…but the clock was also ticking for Wally. He had to race Merlin to wherever the wizard was going, try to get to Ariane while he was there. Once she knew Aunt Phyllis was safe, she could use her powers to escape.

One night in a nice hotel, Wally thought. *One night. We can spare one night, for Aunt Phyllis, and for me.*

He took a deep breath to try to slow his racing heart,

and carried on to the room.

"Hi, Aunt Phyllis," he said as he entered. "How about we order dessert from room service?"

Two hours later, Aunt Phyllis was in her bed, and Wally, the piece of pie he'd eaten sitting rather uneasily in his stomach on top of the pizza he'd had in Prince Albert, was lying fully dressed on his. *Rex Major's men won't come knocking in the middle of the night,* he told himself as he lay there, staring up in the darkness. *You're being silly.*

But sleep was a long time coming just the same.

◄► ►

A prickle of magic woke Merlin in the middle of the night. He blinked up at the dim-lit ceiling, then sat up, frowning. *Wally,* he thought.

The magic told him Wally had come in contact with one of his networks, but he couldn't tell which one. He just sensed the boy's presence in his mind, as though he had come into the room. *I wish he was in the room,* he thought as he got up and pulled on the robe he had left at the foot of the bed. *It would make it easier to strangle him.*

He sat at his desk then opened a program his IT gurus would have been utterly bewildered to see, since only part of it involved the usual sort of computer operations conducted by countless on-off switches and a connection to the Internet, while the rest involved the tug and flow of magic and a connection to the frustratingly thin trickle of power he received from Faerie. From their point of view, it would have seemed to do nothing at all. But for him...

A globe appeared, a representation of the Earth. It spun until the western hemisphere was front and centre. The view zoomed down until Canada filled the screen. Major tugged again with his magic, expecting the view to zoom to southern Ontario, and then on down into the city of Toronto.

Except it didn't. Instead, it zoomed in on Saskatchewan…then down to the city of Saskatoon.

He had tendrils of magic in networks all over the city, but the one that had brushed up against Wally was one he had used before, when he needed to find someone – as in his recently launched search for the whereabouts of Ariane's mother, who had refused the Lady's power and thus was no threat to him, but who would certainly be the ultimate hostage to ensure Ariane's further cooperation. Emily Forsythe had remained remarkably elusive, though he had captured a photo of her from a security camera, and it was a security camera network that drew his attention now: not the one where he had found an image of hers, which was connected to a chain of convenience stores, but a much higher-level network, the one used by the Royal Bank of Canada to keep an eye on people using their ATMs.

He zoomed in farther, found the specific ATM: the main branch of the bank, right in the heart of downtown. He clicked buttons that would have been dead links to anyone else, and an image appeared: Wally Knight, in Saskatoon, using an ATM some hours before. *But where is he now?*

His magic couldn't tell him. If Wally had used any other computer networks, his magic did not reach them.

He's on the run, he thought. *He thinks the police are after him because of what he did to the guard in the condo. And he's run back to the province he knows best, but not to his hometown, because he doesn't want to be recognized.*

The bank's internal network for managing money was not, unfortunately, something he could access, so he couldn't see exactly what Wally had been doing at the

ATM, but he could guess: taking cash out of his account so he could keep running without leaving a paper trail for anyone to follow.

He said he'd be checking email, Major thought. He opened his email program, sent a note. *Wally, I know you're in Saskatoon. You don't have to keep running. Everything is settled back in Toronto. Call my cell phone and I'll arrange for you to go back to my condo. There's nothing to worry about. RM.* He clicked *Send*, then frowned at the screen a moment longer before getting up and going back to bed.

I hope the brat doesn't get himself into any serious scrapes while I'm away, he thought. Then he chuckled a little. *Although he is Arthur's heir. It's not like Arthur didn't get himself into – and out of – far more serious scrapes than anything Wally is likely to fall into.*

The brat'll be fine. He rolled onto his side and closed his eyes. *And once I have the entire sword...*

He let that pleasant thought take him back into sleep.

CHAPTER ELEVEN

TRAVEL PLANS

WALLY JERKED AWAKE TO A NOISE in the hallway. He sat up.

Grey light was beginning to creep into the room around the edges of the thick curtain. Aunt Phyllis still slept. He felt grimy, and his skin felt as rumpled as his clothes after sleeping in them all night.

What had he heard?

He got up, crept to the door, and pressed his ear against it.

"...have to hurry if we're going to..." the voice faded toward the elevators.

Wally took a deep relieved breath, and then turned back to the room. "Aunt Phyllis," he said.

She muttered, but didn't wake.

He went over closer to her, leaned over. "Aunt Phyllis."

Her eyes fluttered open. For a moment she looked confused and frightened and so aged and frail that Wally thought his heart would break. But then her old spirit somehow came flooding back into her face, and she smiled. "Good morning, Wally," she said. "Is it time to get up?"

He nodded. "I think we should leave as soon as we

can," he said. "I'm afraid Rex Major may figure out we're here." He jerked his thumb at the door. "I'm going back down to the business centre to see if his pilot has filed a flight plan yet."

"That will tell you where *you're* going," Aunt Phyllis said. She sat up, and scooted back against the headboard. "But where am *I* going?"

Wally shook his head. "I don't know," he admitted. Which was a pretty glaring hole in his plans, now that he thought of it. He'd pictured them just checking into a hotel in Saskatoon, where Aunt Phyllis could stay comfortably while he went haring off after Major and Ariane. But if Major really did know where they were...

"I have a suggestion, then," Aunt Phyllis said. "I have an old friend in Estevan whom I don't see often enough. She's been wanting me to come stay with her for ages, but it's simply been too difficult because of having to look after Ariane."

Wally's heart leaped. "It would be awfully short notice," he said. "Would she really let you just...show up?"

"I'm sure if I phone her from here, tell her Ariane is away on a...a school trip...and I have a few days free, she would be delighted."

"Aunt Phyllis, that sounds perfect," Wally said, immensely relieved. "As long as you stay off the Internet and are careful about staying away from places with security cameras, Rex Major will have a very hard time figuring out where you are. I'll check the bus schedule right now while I'm at the computer."

"And I'll get dressed," Aunt Phyllis said.

Wally, after a detour to the bathroom for a quick shower, headed downstairs a few minutes later, hair wet but feeling much more human than he had when he'd first woken up. He sat down at the business centre terminal and checked his email first. His heart thumped when he saw that one was from Rex Major...but he was grinning after he'd read it.

Major knew he was in Saskatoon, but clearly didn't know *where*. And he still thought Wally was running from the events in Toronto, which meant he hadn't heard about Aunt Phyllis's escape yet. Major wanted him to call. That meant he was unlikely to have anyone actively searching for Wally in Saskatoon, at least not yet. And that meant they really did have a chance to spirit Aunt Phyllis away.

Wally considered Rex Major's email. His grin widened. *He wants me to call him*, he thought. *Wally Knight, how good of an actor are you?*

Good enough, he decided, and reached for the phone.

◂ ▸

Rex Major had left Faerie more than a millennium ago, had lived a long life in the era of Arthur, had spent hundreds of years trapped in time within the hollow tree where Viviane had imprisoned him, watching the decades flit past. He had lived in this era many years more. And yet...when he dreamed, it was always of Faerie, of the palace where he had grown up with his sister, now the Lady of the Lake, of his parents, who had long since vanished from the land of the living, of plants and animals and music and food that did not exist on Earth and that he had not seen or heard or tasted in centuries.

It was from just such a dream, a pleasant one, that the sound of the cell phone woke him. He blinked up at the ceiling of the hotel room for a moment, the sweet lingering notes of an ancient song played on an instrument humanity had no word for fading from his mind, and then rolled over and picked up the phone.

"Hello, Mr. Major," said Wally Knight.

The last shreds of the dream blew out of his mind like

clouds before a hurricane. Major sat up in bed. "Wally," he said. "Where are you?"

"In Saskatoon," Wally said. "In a hotel. I had some money and I didn't know where else to stay. I checked my email and saw…is it really all right? I didn't kill that guard?"

"No," Major said. "Of course not. Gave him a nasty bump and a cut that needed a couple of stitches, that's all. No worse than what Ariane did to you in France, really. You didn't need to run."

"I thought I did," Wally said. He sounded relieved. "I really thought I'd killed him. And I was scared…I don't even know how I did it. I'm not a fighter! But somehow…" He hesitated. "Does it have something to do with…with whatever you suspect about me? The secret you haven't told me yet?"

"Yes," Major said. "I think it does. But we need to find out for sure. I need you to go home, Wally. I'm tied up on business…I'm in Vancouver, by the way…but I'll be home in three or four days at most. I want you waiting for me. Then I can finally make sure that you're whom I think you are."

A long silence. "Okay," Wally said. "I'm sorry, Mr. Major. I didn't mean to cause so much trouble. I just wanted to go out and I thought I'd just push the guy and run past him into the elevator. But…"

"I understand," Major said, filling his voice with (entirely phony) warmth and understanding. "I completely understand, Wally. It's all right."

"Thank you," Wally said in a small voice. Another long pause. "Have you…heard anything about Ariane? Is she all right?"

Major didn't even glance at the open door into Ariane's room. "I haven't heard anything," he said. "I'm sorry, Wally."

Wally didn't reply.

"Cheer up," Major continued. "I'm sure she's fine. Wally, I'm going to buy you a ticket back to Toronto. I'll email you the information so you can check in. I'll send a limo to meet you at the airport. Deal?"

"Deal," Wally said.

"Good," Major said. "Excellent." He felt relieved to have the matter of Wally settled before he and Ariane headed to New Zealand. "As I said, I'll be home in a few days, and then I'll be able to tell you the big secret. Okay?"

"Okay," Wally said. "I'll be waiting. Bye."

"Bye."

Wally hung up. Major checked the time. *Too late to go back to sleep*, he thought. *Let's get the day started. A passport for Ariane...and then off to New Zealand for the third shard.*

He called his pilot, told him to file a flight plan for Queenstown, New Zealand, departing that evening, and then got out of bed.

It's going to be a great day, he thought, and headed to the shower.

◀ ▶

That went well, Wally thought, grinning to himself as he hung up the phone. *That went remarkably well.* He remembered a line he'd read in a book sometime: *the wicked are always surprised that the good can be clever.*

He could tell he'd woken Major from sleep, which made him rather childishly glad. However, it meant Major probably hadn't told his pilot anything about their plans yet. All the same, he checked the website he'd looked at the night before. Nothing had been added since the flight plan from Prince Albert to Vancouver from the previous day. *I'll get Aunt Phyllis on the bus and then check again.*

He went back up to the room. Aunt Phyllis was dressed

and sitting on the bed. "Rex Major thinks I'm going to fly quietly back to Toronto," he said. "He still doesn't know about you."

"How do you know?" Aunt Phyllis said.

"I talked to him," Wally said.

Aunt Phyllis's hand flew to her mouth. "Really? Wally, that's dangerous! His magic…"

"It doesn't work on me," Wally said. "He told me so himself. He can't make me do what he tells me to do. I don't know why." His only regret about not taking Major up on the offer to fly back to Toronto was that he was passing up his final chance to learn the deep dark secret about himself. "Anyway, he's in Vancouver. He claims he still hasn't heard anything about Ariane, but we know she's with him. I don't know yet where he's going. So let's get you safely off to Estevan…and then I'll see what I can find out."

"Can we start with breakfast?" Aunt Phyllis said. "I'm famished."

Wally's stomach rumbled. "Absolutely," he said. "Breakfast."

◄◄ ►►

The next bus to Regina left at 1:15 p.m. Aunt Phyllis would have to spend an hour and a half in Regina before leaving for Estevan at 5:30, arriving at 8:15. After breakfast in the hotel dining room, they'd walked over to the bus depot, where Wally bought the tickets with cash. Aunt Phyllis had already phoned her friend in Estevan, who was delighted she was coming and hoped she'd stay as long as she could.

They waited at the bus depot, eating lunch in the Robin's Donuts located there. Shortly after 1 p.m., feeling as if a huge weight had been taken off his shoulders, Wally watched Aunt Phyllis board the bus. He'd promised to keep her posted – she'd given him her friend's telephone number. He just hoped Rex Major would have a hard time finding her down in Estevan, because sooner or later the sorcerer would discover she had slipped his grasp, with Wally's help, and then he'd be after her again: she was the only way he had of keeping Ariane in line.

Of course, even after Major learned the truth, he wouldn't tell Ariane. His leverage over her would hold only as long as she thought he held Aunt Phyllis. So Wally's next trick would be flying halfway around the world, catching up with Major and Ariane without Major finding out about it, and somehow getting word to Ariane that Aunt Phyllis was safe without Major preventing it.

Which meant he needed a computer.

He couldn't go back to the hotel, since they'd checked out, but the public library was open and an easy walk from the bus depot. He found an open workstation next to a window and, keeping one eye on the street just in case a black SUV suddenly pulled up, full of private-security goons with kidnapping on their minds, checked the flight-tracking website.

This time, he hit pay dirt. Major's pilot had filed his flight plan. He would leave Vancouver at 8 p.m. that evening to fly to Honolulu.

After his first burst of elation, Wally's heart sank. He doubted he could even start his journey until the morning flights out of Saskatoon. There was no way he could catch them.

Except...

He looked closer. The date for Rex Major to fly out of Honolulu wasn't tomorrow. It was the day after. For whatever reason – business, Wally guessed – Rex Major was stopping in Hawaii for more than a day.

And when he left, he was flying to Queenstown, New

Zealand, arriving early in the afternoon.

Queenstown, Wally thought. *I've got to get to Queenstown before Rex Major.*

He called up a travel-planning site, and checked available flights.

He would have to leave at 7:45 the next morning. The first leg would take him to Calgary. He would wait there for almost four hours, then fly on to Los Angeles. He'd be stuck there seven hours, leaving at 9 p.m. for an overnight flight that would put in him Auckland at 7 a.m. the next day...or kind of the day after that, since they'd cross the International Date Line, but whatever. Then another three hours and he'd leave for Queenstown. New Zealand required foreigners without a visa to have a return flight booked before they could even enter the country, so he'd book the return for five days later. Whatever was going to happen would surely have happened by then. The total cost was around $3,000, but Aunt Phyllis had left him her credit card and told him it had more than $3,500 available on it. So he could afford it. And thanks to that mysterious layover in Hawaii, he would get to Queenstown before Rex Major, by a couple of hours at least.

After that...

After that, he'd have to play it by ear.

He snorted. *As opposed to the detailed planning I've been doing so far.*

He sighed. Looked as though he was stuck in Saskatoon for another night. *Back to the hotel?*

But then he frowned as a thought struck him. By the next morning, Major would know he hadn't flown to Toronto. In fact, he'd know later that afternoon. And probably by the time he discovered that, he would have checked on Aunt Phyllis and discovered she'd been freed. By the time Wally was due to fly out, Major would be on high alert.

No security goons in a black SUV had pulled up outside the library, but he'd be willing to bet they'd be waiting for him at the airport by tomorrow morning. Especially since he was now going to have to book his ticket to New Zealand. Major might not be looking for his name in airline databases right *now*, but he would be the minute he heard Wally had not used the ticket to Toronto – even if he hadn't heard about Aunt Phyllis.

Now that he thought about it, he *couldn't* go back to the hotel. He was a minor. He wasn't sure he could even *try* to check into a hotel without running the risk of the cops being called. And he couldn't exactly sleep on the street – he'd had no practice at being homeless and didn't want to start now.

But the airport was open twenty-four hours. And if he was already *in* the airport, there was no way Major's men, even if they were looking for him and even if they spotted him, could keep him from getting on his airplane.

Aunt Phyllis was safely out of the way. He knew where Merlin was headed. He had a fighting chance of getting there first. He had no one to answer to but himself.

A night in the airport didn't sound like fun. Especially not when it was to be followed by almost a day and a half of travelling and more hours spent in airports. *That which does not kill me makes me stronger*, he reminded himself. *So I should be really strong when I get to New Zealand.*

Also really smelly.

He sighed. *Better get a taxi.*

As he got into a cab outside the library a few minutes later, though, he did smile at the thought that their quest for the shards of Excalibur was about to land Ariane and himself in the stand-in for Middle Earth itself, New Zealand.

If Elijah Wood and Martin Freeman can pull off impossible quests in New Zealand, so can I, he told himself.

Although they'd had the advantage of reading the scripts first. He didn't even have a chance to rehearse. *And if I ever* do *meet the writer of this particular quest tale*, he thought as the cab pulled away from the library, *I've got a few choice things to say.*

He settled back for ride to the airport. His long, long journey to redeeming himself in Ariane's eyes had finally begun.

◄◄ ►►

Ariane awoke to the sound of the door being opened. She looked sleepily over to the right, to see Rex Major, dressed in his usual impeccable grey business suit, turning from the door with a plastic clothes bag bearing the hotel's logo in his hand. The morning light streaming through the window struck a spark of red fire from the ruby stud in his earlobe as he walked over to the chair on the other side of the bed and placed the clothes bag on it. "Your clothes are clean," he said. "Get up, get dressed. We have to get to the passport office as soon as it opens and we have to get your passport photo taken first."

He went out, though he left the door open. Nervously aware of that open door at her naked back, Ariane slipped out from under the covers, the room's refrigerated air cold on her bare skin, unzipped the bag, and with great relief pulled on her clothes. Then she went into the bathroom and made use of all the other toiletries she'd requested the night before. Feeling much more human, she emerged to find Rex Major waiting impatiently. "Put your shoes on," he said. "We have to go."

She had the strong urge to dawdle just to annoy him, but she wasn't four years old anymore, so she pulled on her socks and shoes at the usual speed and then followed him out into the hallway and down to the elevators, and thence to the waiting limousine in front of the hotel that took them downtown...albeit slowly, through the worst traffic she'd ever seen in her life. *Vancouver traffic is not like Regina traffic*, she thought.

At the photographer's, she wondered what would happen if she casually mentioned that Rex Major was holding her aunt hostage and had forced her to fly halfway across the country with him and had every intention of taking her halfway around the world...it would be a scandal, Major would be disgraced, and then...

...and then the men he had waiting in the quarry back in Prince Albert would hurt Aunt Phyllis. And Major would still be in control, because of his damnable ability to Command people by magic.

In fact, it wouldn't even get that far, Ariane thought bitterly. *He'd just tell whomever I told to forget the whole thing.*

Defeated before she'd even tried to fight, she sat sullenly through the process of photos – which worked well, since you weren't allowed to smile for them – and then, at the passport office, the filling out of forms. She saw Rex Major lean forward and whisper something to the clerk, who blinked and then nodded. He came back to her. "There's no problem with your lack of documentation," he said. "And I have it on good authority that even though we would normally have to wait until tomorrow to get a rush passport, they will be sending *yours* out by courier before the office closes tonight. Which means we can be on our way to New Zealand by 8 p.m. as planned."

"Yay," Ariane said.

"We'll wait at the hotel," Major said.

And that was that. If she had been going to do anything to stop him, it would have had to have been during the trip to get her passport. And she'd done nothing. She *could* do nothing. She was helpless, and trapped, and she didn't even have Wally to help her...because Wally had betrayed her.

Still think that was for my own good, Wally? she thought. But she didn't even have the small satisfaction of being able to tell him that in person.

◄ ►

Ariane's passport arrived at the hotel shortly after 5 p.m. Two and a half hours later, Major led the girl aboard his jet for the second time. This time the flight would be much longer: four and a half hours to Honolulu just to start. He hated the fact they would then have to wait more than a day before continuing on to New Zealand, but business was business, and not all of it could be conducted remotely.

Although *some* of it could. "Make yourself comfortable," he told Ariane. "I have to make some phone calls."

Ten minutes after he'd settled himself at his desk, the pilot's voice came over the intercom, telling both passengers to strap in. Major buckled the belt built into his seat and continued working. Once he'd caught up on email he checked the time. The first flight back to Toronto he'd been able to get Wally on had left Saskatoon less than an hour ago. He'd have to check in with his men in Toronto about halfway through his own flight to Honolulu to make sure the boy had done what he was told.

But he could check in with his men in Prince Albert now. He called up the number for Frank LaFebvre, his contact at Ochrana Security.

Frank answered at once. "Ochrana Security, Frank speaking."

"Hi, Frank, it's Rex Major," Major said. He was multitasking, calling up the balance sheet for his fledgling games division while he talked. "Everything all right?"

"Yes, sir," Frank said. "Everything went smoothly."

"That's good…" Major said absently, and then frowned. *Wait, what?* "What do you mean, everything went smoothly? All you have to do is keep Phyllis tucked away."

"And we did, sir," Frank said. "As requested."

"Good," Major said. He scrolled through the spreadsheet. "Good."

"Right up until you sent that boy for her."

Major's finger froze on the mouse wheel. "What? What boy?"

"Wally Knight," Frank said, sounding puzzled. "You emailed us, said he would be coming to pick up Phyllis. He showed up right on schedule and took her away. We've already cleaned up the site and returned the camper."

Major heard a distant roaring that had nothing to do with the sound of the jet taking off, just as the sudden weight on his chest had nothing to do with the acceleration pushing him back into his seat. Wally Knight had betrayed him. Lied to him. To *him*, Merlin. Not only that, he'd clearly hacked into his email account. Who knew what damage he had done?

"When was this?" he asked, fighting to betray nothing of his fury in his voice – and succeeding: Major was very good at hiding his true feelings. It was one reason he had succeeded both as the power behind the throne of Camelot and as a modern businessman.

"Yesterday evening, sir," Frank said. "Around five o'clock, just as the sun was setting."

When Wally called me last night, he had already stolen Aunt Phyllis, Major thought, the rage in him burning ever hotter. *He's not on the plane to Toronto. He could be anywhere by now. And so could the old woman.*

"Frank," Rex Major said, and maybe he *did* let a little bit of what he was feeling into his voice, because he heard Frank LaFebvre's sharp intake of breath, "Wally Knight did not have my authorization to take Aunt Phyllis away. The email you received was a trick."

"Sir?" Frank said. "I'm sorry, there was no way –"

"I'm not blaming you," Rex Major said, though he wanted too very much, so he'd have *someone* to punish in lieu of Wally, "but I need you to make it right. Find out where Wally went. Find out where Phyllis went. Find them both. And let me know the minute you have either one of them."

"Yes, sir," Frank said.

Major disconnected. He stared at the spreadsheet.

The only reason Ariane is helping me is because she thinks I've got her Aunt Phyllis, he thought. *If she finds out the truth while she has the second shard…*

She won't. She can't. How could she? There's no way for Wally to know where we're going. There's no way for him to contact Ariane. She will retrieve the shard and give it to me, and then I will force her to give me the first shard, as well, and with three shards completely in my power, neither she nor the boy can threaten my power again.

He frowned. He still had a use for Wally, the heir of Arthur, though.

Then he smiled, because once Ariane was neutralized as a threat, she would still make an excellent hostage. Just as she would do anything to protect her Aunt Phyllis, Wally would do anything to protect her. He'd made that clear often enough.

Love, Major thought. *The downfall of Arthur: had he not loved Guinevere, Lancelot's betrayal could never have happened, and his kingdom would not have been so divided and weak that it fell to Mordred and his rebels.*

Major was no stranger to love, but his love was not for any one woman or man. What he loved, the *only* thing he loved, was his world of Faerie, and especially his home demesne of Avalon. He wanted it to be as great as it once was, as great as it *could* be.

He had never loved his parents, who had vanished from his life shortly after he was born, secretly executed, he believed, by the Queen. He had been fond of his sister, but their rivalry had begun very early, and now he felt nothing but anger and contempt toward her. Love would never be *his* downfall. But it would be Wally Knight's. Once Ariane had done what he needed her to do, then he would make Wally's love for her into a leash the boy could never cut himself loose from, until he had served Merlin in the conquest of Earth and the liberation of Faerie.

He took a deep breath, and then returned to the financial spreadsheet. But a thought lingered in the back of his mind.

And if Wally Knight doesn't work out...there may be one other possibility.

It felt good to have a back-up plan. He tucked the sudden notion into the back of his mind to examine later, and bent to his work.

CHAPTER TWELVE

UP IN THE AIR

WHEN MAJOR EMERGED FROM HIS OFFICE an hour into the flight, Ariane sensed at once that something had happened to trouble him. She wasn't sure how she knew: there was nothing in his expression or bearing that told her. And yet she knew.

Some sense of the Lady's? she wondered. *I have one shard with me and one hidden away. And he and the Lady are brother and sister, after all.*

"Anything wrong?" she asked, trying to sound nonchalant, although considering her situation that was perhaps not the most believable emotional state to strive to project.

"Nothing at all," Major said. "Why do you ask?"

She shrugged. "Just making conversation. And you look tense."

"I have a lot of responsibilities," he said shortly. "Are you sleepy? Please feel free to use the bedroom at the back of the plane."

"It's only nine o'clock by the time we left," Ariane pointed out. "I don't go to bed at nine."

Major shrugged. "Suit yourself." He sat down opposite her, and pulled the book that had been resting on the bench-like seat toward him. Ariane had looked at it while he was busy in the office. Entitled *Competitive Strategy: Techniques for Analyzing Industries and Competitors*, it hadn't seemed her cup of tea.

But there was nothing else to read on the plane that she'd been able to find. No magazines, no newspapers, and certainly no thick fantasy novels of the kind she'd always favoured. The plane did boast an elaborate entertainment system, but there was absolutely no content to watch or listen to. Sure, there was plenty of food and drink, but she could hardly fill her time chowing down on Pringles and Coke, and she'd already nixed the idea of getting drunk on little bottles of whisky during the flight to Vancouver.

"What happens when we get to New Zealand?" she said at last, both to pass the time and to try to figure out what to expect.

"We land," Major said. "We get off the plane. You try to home in on the third shard. You find it. You retrieve it. You give it and the second shard to me of your own free will." He smiled thinly at that. "And then we fly back to Canada and you take me to where you hid the first shard. Once I have three of the five shards, I will easily find the others. You've already lost, Ariane...or should I say, my dear sister the Lady of the Lake has lost. We just have to go through the motions now."

"Anybody ever tell you you're crappy company on a long flight?" Ariane muttered. She got to her feet. "Maybe I will take a nap, after all."

"Sweet dreams," Major said, but he already had his nose in the book.

Ariane, fuming, made her way to the bedroom at the back. She used the larger-than-usual lavatory just beyond it, then went into the bedroom and closed the door. Besides the twin-sized bed and a barely-there side table, the only furnishing was a leather-upholstered chair built into the aft bulkhead. *Wally must have slept in here on the way back from France*, she thought as she sat on the edge of the bed. She kicked off her shoes and swung her stockinged feet up onto the bed. *After he betrayed me.*

Hot tears welled in her eyes and she dashed them away with the back of her hand. *Not enough water to be useful*, she thought bitterly. *And salt, at that.*

There had to be a way out of the trap Merlin had locked her into. There had to be a way to take the third shard for herself, flee back through the clouds to Canada, retrieve the first shard. That would give *her* three. With three, Major wouldn't have a chance. She'd have the power to go anywhere in the world to retrieve the fourth and then the fifth shards. Major would be left sputtering and impotent, and she would rule in his...

She caught herself as that thought surfaced. *Rule?* she thought. *I don't want to rule. I just want to stop him from ruling.*

But with the sword re-forged, with all the power stored in the shards united and amplified, what could she do? Or maybe the right question was, what *couldn't* she do? Without a shard, she'd toppled a mining shovel. With one shard, she'd flown singlehandedly across the Atlantic, and unlike Charles Lindbergh, hadn't needed an airplane to do it. With Excalibur whole and in her hand, she could do whatever she wanted.

Including crossing to Faerie herself and delivering Excalibur into the hands of the Lady of the Lake.

That thought made her blink, because it didn't feel at all like one of her own. It felt like it had come from *outside* her, like someone was trying to order her, or at least influence her, to do something he or she wanted done, rather than what she chose to do.

The Lady? she thought. *Is she still trying to get her*

claws into me through the tiny opening between her world and Earth?

Well, that's a creepy thought, she thought. Then she frowned. Wally had expressed doubts as to the Lady's trustworthiness. Could he have been right all along?

She snorted. Even if he was, it didn't follow that *Rex Major* was the trustworthy one.

Maybe we shouldn't trust either of them, she thought. *Maybe the only people we can trust are ourselves.*

But then she remembered how the power had seized her and made her throw Flish and her friends around like dolls on the tennis court, and the black thought settled in her heart that maybe she couldn't even trust herself.

I wish none of this had ever happened. I'd rather be the bullied foster kid than the Lady of the Lake. I wish... I wish...

If wishes were horses, beggars would ride, ran the old cliché. No matter what she wished, it would not change reality – not without a genie's lamp at hand.

All she could do was continue to muddle along the best she could, looking for a way to thwart Major's plans. Once he was neutralized, she'd have time enough to worry about the Lady.

And Wally? the thought came unbidden.

She thrust it away. *Let Wally worry about himself*, she though bitterly. *That's what he's good at.*

She lay back on the bed, but whether it was because it still wasn't very late or for other reasons, she did not sleep.

◄► ◄►

Wally had never been more exhausted in his life. It was 3 a.m. and he'd been in the airport since mid-afternoon. The security guards had approached him after he'd been there four hours or so, but he'd shown them his boarding pass for the morning flight and they'd shrugged and let him stay. He'd drunk as much Tim Horton's coffee as he could. He'd eaten two meals. He'd bought a fantasy novel from the gift shop – the cover, featuring a copper-coloured mask studded with rubies, had caught his eye – and read half of it. The fifteen-year-old heroine in it had faced way more danger than he had, which made him feel better. On the other hand, every decision *she* made seemed to make things *worse*. He decided she wasn't much of a role model.

He'd dozed, changed seats, dozed some more. He thought the night would never end.

He was heading to the bathroom when he saw Frank from Ochrana Security standing just inside the main doors to the terminal, staring up and down the brightly lit but almost empty hall. Two other big suit-clad men flanked him. With a flick of his hand he dispatched one toward the luggage-retrieval area, and the other toward Wally.

His first instinct was to hide. But then he remembered where he was. What was Frank going to do? Haul him kicking and screaming out of the terminal? That would bring the security guards running and the police would follow up soon after. Very awkward questions would be asked, involving who had hired Frank and why a private-security firm was kidnapping children from airports.

And so Wally went into the bathroom as he'd intended, and when he came out, walked down to where Frank stood and gave him a cheery wave. "Hi again," he said. "Are you looking for me?"

Frank was wearing dark glasses, apparently oblivious to the fact it made him look either like a Secret Service agent in a Hollywood movie or someone with an eye infection. He stared at Wally as though he couldn't believe he was talking to him. "You lied to me," he growled. "And Mr. Major isn't happy about it."

"Didn't think he would be," Wally said cheerfully. "What is he going to do about it?"

"You're coming with me," Frank said.

Wally glanced over his shoulder. A security guard was watching them, just as he'd expected. Not to mention who knew how many cameras. "Really?" he said. "Because I don't see why I should."

Frank glanced at the guard. "I'll tell him I'm your father."

"I'll tell him you aren't," Wally said. "Which will be easy enough to prove. Especially since my father is a well-respected businessman in Regina. Rex Major may be *way* richer, but he doesn't have any Saskatchewan office towers named after him. Or advertise on the big screen at 'Rider games. Or give generously to the Regina Symphony Orchestra and Globe Theatre. Or…"

Frank's frown turned into a scowl. "You can't hide in here forever."

"I'm not hiding," Wally said, which was both true and not true. He wasn't hiding now, but he had been up until five minutes ago. "I'm just waiting for my flight."

"Where to?" Frank said.

Wally laughed. "Why would I tell you?"

"Mr. Major can find out."

Wally shrugged. "Let him."

Frank stared at him. Wally gave the big man his most insolent grin, the one he'd been told to wipe off his face more than once by authority figures – and a *lot* more than once by his sister.

Frank's compatriots were converging on them. He glanced at them, glanced at the security guard, then said, "Let's go," to the others, and led them out.

The guard came over. "Everything all right, kid?" he said.

"Abso – solutely," Wally said, around a yawn that

threatened to swallow the word. Now *that* was over, he felt more exhausted than ever. "Just some friends coming to say goodbye."

"At 3:30 in the morning?" the guard said skeptically.

Wally shrugged. "They do shift work. Start at four. Only time they could come see me off." Inspiration struck. "That's why I've spent the night hanging around."

The guard shook his head. "It'd kill me," he said. "But I'm not as young as you are."

Wally was feeling about twenty years older than usual, if truth be told, but he nodded. The guard went back to his station. Wally turned to face the terminal's big glass windows and saw the black SUV he remembered from the quarry driving away in the early-morning darkness. Frank was presumably already on the phone to Rex Major, who had probably already landed in Honolulu.

He found a bench and settled down to wait some more. *Half a day in an airport*, he thought. *And here I thought magical quests were supposed to be exciting.*

Could Rex Major find out where he was flying to? Wally didn't know for sure, but that was the way to bet. *Still*, he thought, *as long as I stay in public areas in airports, he can't do anything. Not in Calgary, not in Los Angeles, not in Queenstown.*

And once he was in Queenstown?

I've got a long flight ahead, he thought. *I'll figure it out as I go. Play it by ear.*

He snorted. Once, just once, he'd really like to have the sheet music.

◄◄ ►►

Rex Major's private jet had left Vancouver at 8 p.m. and landed in Honolulu at just after 12:30 a.m. Vancouver time – 10:30 p.m. Hawaii time. Customs was quickly dealt with: Major was frequently in Hawaii, and well-known to the customs agents there.

He flew there not only to get away from Toronto's winters (although that wasn't a completely trivial reason – he'd often wished the original doorway from Faerie hadn't led to cold and rainy England; the climate in his native Avalon was more like San Diego's), but also because Hawaii was home to the United States Pacific Command (a.k.a. USPACOM – the military loved its acronyms). He was working closely with the U.S. military to integrate his new super-secure Excalibur server software into their systems, all in the name of making sure enemies couldn't hack into it, of course. He'd had similar meetings with the Canadian military and the other members of NATO. What they didn't know was that his clandestine agents were also selling his software, albeit under a different name and apparently originating from a rival company in Moscow, to less savoury nations. All of that software contained threads of Merlin's magic. When Excalibur was reforged and his power came surging back stronger than it was even in Arthur's heyday, he would be able to use that software to seize control of the bulk of the world's armed forces – including, most importantly, *every nuclear missile*. And with his soothing, Commanding Voice spread worldwide by mass media and the Internet, the people of the world would soon be lining up to serve his glorious cause.

Hence the full-day layover in Hawaii. Finding the third shard of Excalibur was crucial to his plans, but so was nailing down his deal with the military.

He'd booked himself a room in an airport hotel. This time Ariane would have to stay aboard the plane. He couldn't take her with him to USPACOM headquarters for his meetings and he didn't dare leave her where she would have access to a telephone or the Internet in case Wally somehow managed to track her down and get a message to her about the rescue of Aunt Phyllis. He'd called ahead and a guard had already come aboard the plane.

"I'm in Hawaii, and I'm stuck in this stupid plane for a day and a half?" Ariane said as Major walked past her on the way to the front hatch. "You know I can't do anything as long as you have Aunt Phyllis. What are you scared of?"

"I don't trust you," Rex Major said. "You have two shards of Excalibur, one of them on your person. The sword will try to influence you. It might convince you that it's more important to steal away with it than to save your Aunt Phyllis." He gestured at the luxurious cabin. "There's no water here to speak of, so no matter how tempted you are, you can't act. In a hotel room, you might." He nodded at the guard, a taciturn Hawaiian wearing a floral shirt and khaki pants, with tattoos on top of muscles on top of muscles on his thick arms. "Alika here will keep you company. His name means 'guardian,' by the way. How apt is that?"

Ariane stared at Alika. He stared back. "Oh, yeah, he looks like a barrel of laughs."

"You *are* my prisoner, you know," Major said. "Once that would have meant nights in a cold damp dungeon interspersed with periods of agonizing torture. Count your blessings." He nodded to Alika, who nodded back, and headed down the gangway into the soft tropical night.

His limo delivered him to his hotel, where he intended to go straight to bed so he would be fresh for his meetings in the morning: but while he was brushing his teeth his cell phone rang. He spat out the toothpaste, rinsed his mouth quickly, then went into the room and grabbed his phone from the bedside table. "Rex Major," he said. He would have liked to ream out whomever it was for calling him so late, but since the call could be coming

from anywhere in the world, it would have been silly –
it might be noon wherever the call originated.

It wasn't, though. Frank LaFebvre said, "Mr. Major,
we've found Wally."

He came awake. "Where?" he growled.

"Saskatoon airport," Frank said. "He's been there all
day. But we couldn't grab him – too public. He says he's
flying out in the morning. He wouldn't tell me where."

"Not to Toronto, that's for sure," Major said. "Any
sign of Phyllis Forsythe?"

"No," Frank said. "Do you want me to keep looking?"

"Of course I want you to keep looking," Major
snapped. But then he consciously softened his tone. "You
did the best you could with Wally, Frank. I appreciate it.
Be sure to send me your invoice for the work to date. I'll
make sure it gets paid right away. And let me know the
moment you have something on Phyllis."

"Yes, Mr. Major," Frank said. "Thank you."

Major disconnected. He could have told Frank he
wouldn't be paid since he'd been duped so thoroughly, but
not paying the bill would just create an enemy who might
be able to cause him minor difficulty later on. Major liked
to keep focused on the big picture. Well-treated underlings
were typically far more loyal than those whom he coerced
with threatening and punishing.

Not that he was above threatening and punishing if he
thought it would do some good. Threatening and punishing Wally Knight, for instance, he would have enjoyed
very much at that moment.

*If he's flying out, he's bought tickets. Let's see what I
can find out.*

Air Canada was one of the companies that made ex-
tensive use of Rex Major's software. It took him no time
at all to find the thread of Wally's name in the weave of
his magical web, now that he was looking. He swore

when he saw the boy's itinerary.

He knows!

Wally Knight was flying to Queenstown, New Zealand. And because Major had to stay in Honolulu for a day, he would get there first. He'd undoubtedly hang around the airport and try to communicate with Ariane when they arrived, tell her that Aunt Phyllis was safe. Frank was quite right: there was no way to grab the kid from an airport without causing a scene and raising questions whose answers would inevitably and uncomfortably focus attention on Major.

Then he smiled. But there was also no way Wally Knight could gain access to where Major's jet would land, where there would be a vehicle waiting to whisk them away the minute they set down. Wally Knight could watch them drive away, but he'd never know where they went. And a few hours after that, the third shard would be his.

And when Wally did leave the airport...

He checked the time. There was only an hour's difference in time between Honolulu and Queenstown. An hour's difference and an entire day, since Queenstown was on the other side of the International Date Line, but that didn't matter as far as figuring out business hours went. He'd call his people in Queenstown sometime during his day's meetings.

He *would* get Wally back – and then get on with the threatening and punishing he was already looking forward to.

He yawned and went back to getting ready for bed. The next couple of days were going to be busy.

And then, just as he was pulling back the covers, his cell phone dinged, the distinctive sound of an urgent email arriving. He sighed, picked up the phone and read the message. He read it again. Then he smiled.

His magical web had just snared another bit of valuable

information – *extremely* valuable.

He knew where Ariane had hidden the *first* shard. It would still be easiest to have her retrieve it for him, but just in case things went horribly awry...

Mentally adding another item to the next day's to-do list, he put down the cell phone and climbed under the covers.

He was still smiling when he fell asleep five minutes later.

CHAPTER THIRTEEN

WELCOME TO NEW ZEALAND

FLYING IS GREATLY OVERRATED, Wally thought groggily as he blinked bleary eyes at the city of Queenstown through the window of the Air New Zealand Airbus A320. Not that it wasn't a pretty town, set on the shores of the spectacular Lake Wakatipu and surrounded by even more spectacular mountains. It was also surprisingly small: only about twelve thousand permanent residents in the town itself, with maybe another ten thousand in the surrounding Lakes District, according to the research he'd done during the three-hour layover he'd had in Auckland even after clearing customs (where he had invented a doting aunt waiting to show him the sights of New Zealand to take their minds off the suspicious fact he was an almost-fifteen-year-old travelling alone).

It was while he was in Auckland that he'd finally figured out what to do once he reached Queenstown.

All during the long hours, flying from Saskatoon to Calgary to Los Angeles to, finally, Auckland, he'd been mulling it over. He knew from the flight plan filed by Rex Major's pilot that he had a good chance of getting to Queenstown first. But he also knew from the appearance of Frank at the Saskatoon airport that Major knew he was on the loose, and he had to assume Major could access airline computer systems and discover he was flying to Queenstown.

The question was, what would Major do with that information? The answer seemed clear: he'd arrange for someone to try to nab Wally at the airport. They might not be able to grab him in the terminal itself, but he couldn't stay there forever, especially not if he intended to help Ariane, and the minute he set foot outside of it, they'd come after him.

But then Wally had realized: for that to happen, Major would have had to get in touch with someone ahead of time. And since it was unlikely he had private security people at his beck and call *everywhere*, the most likely people for him to contact were his own employees – employees of Excalibur Computer Systems. A little Googling at a public terminal in Los Angeles had shown him that while there wasn't an ECS office in Queenstown, there *was* one in Auckland – the only one in the country, in fact.

A visit to the local office's website had given him the name and email of the manager there, a fellow named Carl Paulsen. He'd smiled as he'd looked at the address. *I knew that secondary email address I set up in Rex Major's name while I was in his computer would come in handy.* Any email he sent using it would still be sent by ECS's servers, would still appear to come from Major – but Major, even if by now he had blocked Wally's access to his main account, would know nothing about the second one unless he went digging. And why would he?

Wally opened up ECS's remote email system and, using the account he'd created, composed a very brief email to the manager in Auckland. *Please confirm arrangements and copy me on all relevant documents at this email address. – RM,* he typed. Then he sent it.

Carl Paulsen would have to be very observant to even notice that the address associated with *this* email from Rex Major was rexmajor@ecs.com, rather than rex.major@ecs.com. And even if he did notice the missing dot, so what? Major might have any number of reasons for having more than one email account.

He didn't have to wait long before the answering email popped up. He grinned as he looked it over. As he'd suspected, Major knew exactly where he was going once he got to Queenstown, and he'd conveyed that information to those making his transportation arrangements. *Driver will be awaiting your arrival at 1:15 p.m.*, the message read. *He will convey you and your companion to Lake Putahi as requested. Two men from our security division will meet the flight from Auckland on which you expect the teenage mule carrying your stolen files to arrive, and will intercept and detain him until you can talk to him. Hope you'll also have time to drop by the Auckland office – I know my staff would love to meet you. Have a safe flight! Carl Paulsen.*

Wally's flight was due to arrive in Queenstown at 12:05. Carl Paulsen's men would be waiting for him, but they didn't know he *knew* they'd be waiting for them. All he had to do was slip past them and grab transportation downtown. After that...

After that, he thought now, as he yawned and straightened his seat back in preparation for landing in Queenstown, *I just have to find this Lake Putahi.*

The Queenstown airport was surprisingly large for such a small town. His stomach grumbled as he came into the terminal, and he felt a rather overpowering need for caffeine, so he stopped at the Patagonia Chocolates stand and ordered ice cream and coffee. Both were delicious. Feeling more human, he tossed the ice cream container into the trash and made his way to the exit...WAY OUT, it read above the door, which he thought was pretty funny.

"Excuse me, son," said a voice behind him, and his heart leaped into his throat. He didn't even turn around. Instead he dashed through the WAY OUT. The voice shouted at him but he grabbed the door of the nearest of the line of taxis waiting for the disembarking passengers and slid into the back seat.

"Lake Putahi," he said to the driver breathlessly.

"Can't do it, mate," the driver said. "That's a special request."

"Then take me to your leader," Wally said. He looked out. There were two big men in suits converging on the taxi. "Now would be good."

The driver pulled away from the curb, leaving the ECS security guys glaring after them. Wally twisted around and saw them running across the road toward the parking lot. No doubt they'd try to follow. But a minute later they were out of sight.

He twisted around again. "Let's take the scenic route," he said. "Down by the lake."

"Suit yourself," the driver said, and turned down into the town. A moment later they were diving through a residential area close to the lakeshore. Wally kept looking behind them, but didn't see anybody following – not obviously anyway.

"Pretty town," Wally said.

"We like it," the driver said. His New Zealand accent sounded strange to Wally. He'd met a few Australians, and this accent was similar, but not identical. He couldn't quite put his finger on the difference. Something to do with the vowels…

"So who were the blokes chasing you back there?" the driver said. "You in trouble, mate?"

Wally blinked. He hadn't realized the driver had noticed. "No," Wally said. "Not really. They work for my father."

The driver laughed. "Slipping the leash, are you?"

"Something like that." He decided to change the subject. "So *can* your company take me to Lake Putahi?"

The driver shrugged. "Sure, mate. For a price."

"I've got the money," Wally said.

"Then talk to the boss."

Wally looked out the back window again. All clear. Then he glanced at his watch. It was 12:30 p.m. local time. He couldn't even begin to figure out what time that was back home. Middle of the night from the way he felt. Or maybe really early morning. Whichever, Rex Major would be landing within the hour, and heading straight to the lake. He needed to get there first.

"Step on it," he said to the driver, and grinned to himself. *I've always wanted to say that to a cabbie.*

But *this* cabbie disappointed him by saying, "Gotta obey the speed limit, mate," and continued at a sedate pace through the quiet neighbourhood. *No driver ever says that in the movies*, Wally thought disgruntedly, but Queenstown – well, technically, this was Frankton, if he remembered the maps he'd looked at correctly, but Frankton was just a suburb of Queenstown – was so small it was still a very few minutes before they pulled up in front of the taxi company's office which, rather to his surprise, was located on a street filled with boutique shops and restaurants. Wally got out and paid the driver, looked up and down the street, and went in to make his rather odd request.

Twenty minutes later he was rolling out of town and heading up into the mountains. It would be very expensive, he'd been warned: Lake Putahi was more than an hour from Queenstown. But he'd paid up front, using the New Zealand dollars he'd exchanged his own Canadian cash for back in Auckland, and that had gone an amazingly long way toward allaying the despatcher's doubts.

The driver didn't say a word, which suited Wally fine. He leaned back in the seat, closed his eyes, and fell instantly asleep.

"Turning off to the lake now," the driver said an indeterminate time later. Wally jerked up and looked around. They were in a steep mountain valley. Low clouds hung on the slopes. They'd obviously climbed a considerable distance since leaving Queenstown, and now they were turning onto a narrow road that wound up toward the hidden mountain peaks. The driver stopped. "Not much of a road up there," he said. "Not much to see, either. Just a parking lot. Not even a picnic bench. Pretty enough lake but not the prettiest, and we've got a lot of lakes in the Lakes District. As you'd expect."

Wally stretched. He'd developed a crick in his neck. "What time is it?"

"Quarter to two."

Rex Major and Ariane were already on the ground and headed his way. The last thing he wanted was for the cab, going down, to meet Major's limo, headed up. "Can I walk up?"

"Bit of a steep go, but yeah. Trail head right over there." The driver pointed out a sign to the left of the road a little farther ahead, where there was a turnout. "Drop you there, then?"

"Please," Wally said.

The driver pulled up to the sign and turned around. Wally got out and took a look at it. It was green with yellow letters. "Lake Putahi, 3.6 km, 1 hour," he read. He hitched his backpack up and buckled the chest strap. He'd have to hurry to get there first. At least it wasn't hot: New Zealand was heading into summer just as Regina was heading into winter, but neither had quite arrived at the next season yet. And the low clouds kept the sun away. If anything, it was on the cool side.

"You right, mate?" the driver said. "Dangerous hiking alone. And looks like it'll be foggy higher up. Could be raining. Not much to see in the fog and rain."

"My dad and sister will be along soon," Wally said. "They're driving up to the lake. I want to surprise them."

The driver shrugged. "Your funeral. I'm off, then." He rolled up the window and drove off in a cloud of dust.

Wally turned his attention to the trail, took a deep breath, and began to climb.

◀◀ ▶▶

Ariane stared out the window of the limousine that had met them at the Queenstown airport. Just before they'd landed, Rex Major had taken a call in his office aboard the jet – a call that clearly had put him in a bad mood. He kept looking around as they walked from the jet to the car as though expecting someone to jump out at them.

There was a second vehicle behind the car, a black Range Rover with two men in it and the Excalibur Computer Systems logo on its doors. Major told Ariane to get in the back seat of the limo, then went over to talk to the men in the Range Rover. She watched him through the car window, wondering what he was saying to them. They simply nodded in response. When the limo pulled away, Ariane, glancing behind, saw the Range Rover was coming with them.

For her part, Ariane was just glad to be off the jet for the first time since Vancouver. It might be a luxurious prison, but it was still a prison.

And there was more. The moment she'd stepped into the open air she'd heard it, with that magical sense that wasn't really hearing but which she interpreted that way: the song of the third shard of Excalibur, anxious to be re-united with its brothers, excited by the nearness of the magic of the Lady of the Lake, who had had it made and brought it to this world. They were definitely in the right place – or close to it, anyway.

They made no side stops in Queenstown. Major's driver immediately headed up into the mountains north of the city. They quickly left the green lake valley behind and were soon winding up steep roads with little traffic. "By all accounts, Lake Putahi is not a particularly popular lake," Major said. "It will most likely be completely deserted. Which is ideal for our purposes, of course."

Ariane said nothing. The shard sang to her, urging her to come to it, to use its power, to join it with the rest of the sword. It hurt to think that she would soon hold it – and then have to hand it over to Major, along with the second shard she wore strapped to her side with the same tensor bandage she normally used for the first, still safely hidden back in Canada.

I'll never give him the first one, she thought. *He may have two, but he won't have three.*

But even as she thought that, she knew it was empty bravado. As long as Major held Aunt Phyllis hostage, she would do whatever he told her to, even *with* the shards urging her to keep them, to use their power to strike him down. She couldn't give in to that call. Nor did she think an attack on Major – on *Merlin* – could succeed. He might not have a lot of magic, but he surely had enough to protect himself against anything she might try. And then he would punish Aunt Phyllis for her niece's temerity.

The shard sang in her head. It was wild and beautiful as always...and knowing what was to come, she hated it.

They drove for an hour before turning off onto a narrow gravel track that climbed up even higher into the mountains. The driver slowed. "Pretty narrow, sir," he said. "Are you sure...?"

"I'm sure," Major snapped. "Drive." He looked at Ariane. "Can you feel it?"

"I can hear it," she said. "Stronger all the time. Ahead of us. It's there."

Major nodded. The expression on his face, grasping, eager, would have made him a prime candidate to play Ebenezer Scrooge – a Scrooge that no mere ghosts of past, present, and future could hope to reform. *He is* the ghost of Christmas past, Ariane thought. *Hundreds of Christmases. I doubt he's celebrated a single one.*

They drove past a green and yellow sign marking the start of a hiking trail to the lake, then began the slow ascent of the switchback road beyond it. Almost as soon as they'd climbed above the valley floor the clouds that had hung over their heads since entering the mountains became fog shrouding them, not so thick they could not see the road, but thick enough they couldn't see anything else, so that they seemed to be climbing into a grey, featureless void where anything might wait for them.

In the end, of course, all that awaited them was a tiny parking lot, empty in the mist. They rolled to a stop with a crunch of gravel. The song of the third shard rang in Ariane's mind like a summoning trumpet. She longed to go to it, but Major growled, "Stay put," and got out, closing the door behind him. She saw him crunch across to the Range Rover and talk to the two men inside. They nodded and got out, then split up, each heading in a different direction around the lake.

Making sure there aren't any witnesses? Ariane thought, but she couldn't figure out why Major would care.

He came back to her. "Get out," he said. "Can you hear it?"

She nodded. She walked to the edge of the water. The song of the shard was almost frantic. She peered into the mist. At the edge of visibility she saw a dark lump, the small island in the middle of the lake she had seen in her dream, a few twisted trees clinging to it, a mound of tumbled rock at its centre. She pointed. "It's out there," she said, her voice sounding thin and strained in her own ears. It was hard to breathe, hard to think with the third shard calling so loudly to her, and with the second shard she wore strapped to her side answering it. "I'll go get it –"

Merlin's hand closed on her arm. "Not yet," he said. He pulled her away from the water. It felt wrong to be moving away from the third shard again.

"What?" she demanded, feeling anger rising in her. "It's right *there*. I can have it in two minutes –"

He held out his hand. "First," he said, "give me the second shard."

She stared at him. "What? Why?"

"Because I don't trust you. Or it." He pointed at her side. "You're already almost hypnotized by the sword. If you have both shards...all three, really, even if you didn't bring the first one with you...I don't think you'll be able to resist its wishes any longer. I think it will force you to flee with it. And that would be unfortunate...for Aunt Phyllis." He met her eyes squarely, his expression stone-like. "You don't want anything bad to happen to her, do you?"

I could vanish into this mist right now, Ariane thought. *I could materialize next to the island, grab the shard, take to the clouds. With two shards, I could fly myself all the way back to Canada. With three shards, I could easily claim the remaining two. I could...*

But she couldn't get back faster than Rex Major could make a simple phone call. And he was holding Aunt Phyllis in a place where there was no water for Ariane to use.

She forced down the anger. Was it even really hers, or was it coming from the sword? It was hard to tell. She pulled up her shirt and unwrapped the tensor bandage, the mist cold on her exposed midriff. She dropped the shirt again and held out the second shard, the one she had stolen from under Major's nose in France, only to have Wally betray her and hand it back to him. Now *she* was the one giving it to him freely.

He took it. His pupils expanded as he touched it, and she knew that in his own way, he felt its power, too. "Good," he said. "Now go. Get the third shard. Bring it back here. And then we will return to Canada and you will give me the first shard, too. Because I still have Aunt Phyllis."

Ariane wanted to attack him, wanted to kick him, bite him, scratch him. Instead, she turned and trudged back to the water. Now she had two shards singing in her head, the one behind her, the one ahead of her, both calling to her. Their songs did not mesh: the only time they had ever meshed perfectly was when Wally, of all people, had held them both. She still didn't understand that.

It didn't matter. She stepped into the water and let it dissolve her, flashing across to the little island in an instant. Dripping, she rose from the lake, waded ashore, and ordered herself dry. She glanced back. She could just see Major in the mist, watching her. To her right the lakeshore was lost in the fog, but to her left, she could see one of the men from the SUV making his way slowly through the rocks and scattered trees, as though searching for something.

The shard was practically screaming at her. She frowned. It seemed to be…down, somehow, inside the pile of rocks at the island's centre. She could see no way through the boulders from this side, so she worked her away carefully around the island's verge, the footing so uncertain between twisted roots and shifting stones that she nearly pitched into the water twice.

The other side of the island, however, had a level space,

almost a beach. There were wet spots on the gravel that spread from there to the tumbled rocks. She frowned at that. *An animal?*

She rounded the rocks. Now she was out of sight of both Major and the man picking his way along the nearer shore. There was a natural opening into the pile of stones. A shadow moved inside it, and her heart suddenly lurched. Did they have bears in New Zealand?

But the pale skinny figure with red hair that climbed out of that hole a moment later, carrying a length of grey metal, ragged at both ends and with an indentation down the middle, was no bear.

Ariane gaped at him. "Wally?" she said, disbelieving. "What are you doing here?" And then she blinked. "And why are you naked?"

CHAPTER FOURTEEN

THE LAKE IN THE CLOUDS

THE SIGN HAD SAID THE TRAIL to Lake Putahi was 3.6 kilometres. By the time he emerged onto the shores of the mist-shrouded body of water he was convinced it was twice that. *Mountains*, he thought, bending over with his hands on his knees, panting. *Why did it have to be mountains? We don't do mountains in Saskatchewan.*

But after a moment or two his heart rate slowed and his breathing was coming easier, so he straightened and looked around him.

Lake Putahi did not look any bigger than Wascana Lake. Smaller, actually, since it was more round and Wascana Lake was really an elongated wide spot in the creek. At least, he thought Putahi wasn't any bigger; he couldn't really see the far shore. He could barely see the parking lot. What he could see was the island in the middle of the lake, and the boulders piled up in the middle of it.

The shard is on that island, he thought. He didn't know *how* he knew. He just knew, somehow, that it wasn't buried in the mud at the bottom of the lake or under a stone near the shore or any of the million other places it could logically have been. It wasn't in any of those places because it was there, on the island.

And then he heard the sound of approaching vehicles, from the direction of the parking lot. Suddenly feeling unpleasantly exposed, he hurried in the opposite direction. There were some large boulders not far away, and he crouched behind them to see who arrived.

It was not a big surprise when the arriving cars proved to be a black limousine and a black SUV. The limo didn't have any insignia, but the black SUV, a Range Rover, had the Excalibur Computer Systems sword-logo on its side.

The door of the limousine opened. Rex Major got out, and as he did so, Wally glimpsed Ariane inside the car. His heart leaped.

He'd seen enough. He knew where the shard was. If he got it first, he could present it to Ariane at the same time as he told her that Aunt Phyllis was no longer a hostage – and maybe, just maybe, she'd forgive him, or at least start to forgive him.

Maybe.

He picked his way carefully along the shore, keeping out of sight of the parking lot, until the mist hid it. Then he hurried. When he had circled the lake to a point where the dark lump of the island was between him and where he judged the parking lot to be, he stopped. The island was closer to the shore at this end, and there was a flat spot on the side facing him that would make it easy to climb out of the water.

The very, very cold water. He could tell that just by looking.

But there was nothing for it.

He hadn't had a lot of swimming lessons, but he could manage a front crawl as far as the island. He just wished he'd brought a swimsuit. *Or a wetsuit*, he thought uneasily, thinking again of how cold the water would be.

But he hadn't come this far to get cold feet. He smirked at his own joke, and then, reasoning that if he moved quickly he wouldn't have time to get cold, he stripped out of his clothes in two minutes flat. Wearing only his undershorts, he stuffed his jeans and T-shirt and shoes and socks into his backpack, took a deep breath, and waded into the water.

It bit at his legs with exactly the icy snap he expected. *In for a penny, in for a pound*, he thought; then, amused at his own turn of phrase, *I read too much British fantasy fiction*; and now he plunged full-length into the lake.

It didn't *quite* take his breath away. He gulped more air anyway and set out for the island, splashily but effectively. It took him five minutes to cross the distance. He hauled himself out onto the flat gravel-covered beach, teeth chattering and limbs shaking. But he had reached the island first. And one look at the mass of rocks at its centre showed him the dark opening that led to where he knew, without a shadow of a doubt, he would find the third shard of Excalibur.

He hurried forward, shivering, and crawled on his hands and knees into the small cave. Inside was a pool, still and clear as crystal. Even in the uncertain light he could see a dark object on the bottom. Lying on his stomach, the rocks pressing into his bare stomach and chest and legs, he reached for it. His fingers touched something hard. He almost had it...he wriggled forward a bit more, and it was in his hand. There were splinters of wood around it, as though it had been in a box, like the one he had seen in Yellowknife when the steam shovel had uncovered the first shard. But the box had long-since disintegrated. *I wonder if that's why there wasn't a box for the second one?* he thought, but the thought was distant. He had the third shard! And as soon as he told Ariane the truth about Aunt Phyllis...

He rolled over, crawled out of the hole, straightened up –

– and saw Ariane staring at him, wide-eyed. "Wally? What are you doing here?" She blinked at him. "And why are you naked?"

"I'm not *naked*," he said indignantly, as best he could between chattering teeth. "I'm wearing shorts."

"Very wet ones," she said. "Practically transparent." He felt himself blushing. "Hold on –" She stepped forward, and suddenly he was dry as a bone, the water exploding from his body in a brief spray.

"Thanks," he said. His mouth was suddenly as dry as the rest of him. He held out the third shard. "I got it for you."

She reached for it. As she took it, for one instant, they were both touching it, and her eyes widened and she gasped a little. Then she snatched it from his hand. She held it up and stared at it. "But I don't understand," she said. "There was no need. Why swim to the island? I was coming to get it anyway."

"I wanted…I wanted to be able to hand it to you. So I –"

"So Rex Major will be proud of you," she said cuttingly. "So you can enjoy watching when I hand it over to him."

He felt like she'd stabbed the shard into his heart. "*No*," he said, desperately. "Major doesn't know I'm here. That's the other reason I swam to the island. I don't want him to see me." Wally wrapped his arms around himself. He was still shivering. Dry was warmer than wet, but the chill mountain mist enveloped them both.

Ariane looked down at the third shard. Longer than either of the first two, cold pitted metal with an indentation down the middle, it gleamed dully in the grey light. "This doesn't change anything, Wally," she said. Her voice sounded dull and defeated, very unlike the girl he remembered. "I don't know what you're playing at, but it doesn't change anything. I have to give it to Rex Major. He has Aunt Phyllis."

"No," Wally said, "he doesn't."

Ariane's head shot up. "What? How do you know?"

"Because I rescued her," Wally said. "I tricked the security guards into handing her over to me. And then I put her on a bus to Estevan. She's safe. You don't have to give Major anything."

Ariane suddenly...well, she didn't really grow, Wally thought, but it seemed like it. She straightened, and seemed to draw power to herself. He blinked. How did he know that? It was as if he was sensing something from the shard, just like Ariane. *But why?* he thought. *What's so special about me?*

He didn't think that after this Major was going to be much inclined to tell him.

"Then let's get out of here," Ariane said. She held up the shard. "I have two again. Major has the second one. He wouldn't let me bring it with me. But I still have the first one. And he doesn't know where I hid it."

There came a shout from the shoreline. Wally shot a glance that way. One of the men from the SUV had come far enough around the shore to see Ariane and Wally standing together on the shore. "We have to go," Ariane said.

"My backpack," Wally said. "My passport. My clothes. On the shore."

Ariane nodded. "Come on." She ran down to the water, Wally close behind. She grabbed his wrist. There was the momentary horrifying feeling of dissolving into nothingness he didn't think he could ever get used to, and then they were clambering out of the icy water onto the shore. Ariane ordered the liquid off of both of them at the same moment there came a shout from the right.

"Stop!"

Not a very original command, Wally thought. He

turned. One of the men from the Range Rover appeared. He had a pistol in one hand...and Wally's backpack, his clothes stuffed roughly into the open top of it, in the other. *Crap!* "Get us out of here!" he cried.

"Not yet," Ariane said quietly. And then, from the water of the lake, Wally saw a sinuous tentacle emerge, like a giant snake.

"Don't move," the man said, pistol aimed at them.

"Don't tell me what to do," Ariane snarled, and the tentacle of water struck. It lashed out faster than any real snake had ever moved, striking the man's wrist. Wally heard a sickening crack and the man, crying out in pain, staggered back, his wrist bent at an unnatural angle. The pistol skittered across the rocks.

Something cracked, a loud, flat sound, and for a second Wally thought the gun had gone off when it was dropped – but he'd read that that was a Hollywood myth: in general, guns don't go off when dropped. Which meant that...

He spun. The second man from the SUV was coming up from behind them, lowering his gun from having fired it into the air. "I don't know how you did that," he growled, "but stay still or –"

But of course it didn't matter if Ariane stayed still or not. She still had her power, and before the second man had finished his command a second tendril of water had smashed down on his wrist. Wally didn't hear a bone break this time, but the gun dropped all the same, and then the same tendril of water lashed around the man's legs and knocked him backward. He thumped to the ground so hard Wally heard the breath whoosh out of him.

Ariane grabbed Wally's hand and pulled him to the water. "Wait!" Wally cried. "My –"

He was going to say, "backpack!", or maybe, "clothes!" but he never got the word out. The water sucked them down, and they left the Lake in the Clouds behind.

◄◄ ►►

Rex Major paced the shore by the parking lot, peering futilely into the mist. He could not sense the shard as strongly as Ariane could, but he knew it was out there. He saw, dimly, Ariane materialize in the water and climb onto the island. He saw her pick her way around the rocks and disappear from view. He waited for her to reappear.

Instead he heard shouts, and then, unmistakably, a gunshot.

What the hell...? Rex Major started running around the shoreline, trying to get a view of the far side of the island. He tripped and fell, ripping the knee of his expensive suit and drawing blood, but he hardly noticed.

What he did notice was that he could no longer sense the shard. Ariane had stolen it after all.

But what about the shot...?

He saw dark figures ahead, resolving into his two employees. As he got nearer he saw that one was grimacing in pain, cradling a wrist that was obviously broken. A blue backpack rested on the ground at his feet. The other was staring around as though looking for something, his gun held loosely in his right hand.

As Major approached, the gun swung up. The man had a panicked look. "Don't shoot, you idiot!" Major snapped. "It's me. What happened?"

"I don't...we saw them...the water..." The man with the broken wrist was pale and clearly in shock to the point of incoherence.

"Quiet!" Major Commanded. He turned to the other one. "Stevens. What did you see?"

"The girl met someone on the island. A boy. In his underwear. They were there, and then somehow... they were climbing out of the water onto the shore. Axel shouted at them, told them to stop, and the water...sir, I know it sounds crazy, but the water...or something in the water, a giant snake of some kind...but that's even crazier...it rose up and smashed his wrist. I came up behind them, fired a warning shot into the air, but then the water hit me, too... knocked my legs out from under me. Then they stepped into the water together and they just...vanished. Like the water sucked them down." He shook his head. "Sir, I swear. I'm not crazy. I'm not drunk. I'm not on drugs. I saw what I saw."

"I believe you," Major said grimly. He glanced at the backpack. He recognized the T-shirt stuffed into it on top of a pair of jeans and some ratty sneakers. *Wally Knight.* The brat had somehow outwitted him, managed not only to get to New Zealand but get to the lake before him. He must have told Ariane the truth about her Aunt Phyllis, and as soon as she knew, she'd felt free to use her power and escape with the third shard.

Good thing I made her leave the second one with me, Major thought. He couldn't use its power while she still held one. He didn't know if she could use the power of the third since she also held the first – which she technically still did, even though she had left it behind. He didn't know if *she* knew. But even drawing on the power of one shard, which was surely all she could manage at best, she would struggle to make it across the Pacific, especially if she tried to travel with Wally. She could never get back before he did.

And he *would* return to Canada. Because he knew something Ariane didn't know he knew: he knew where she had hidden the first shard of Excalibur.

"Forget what really happened here," he Commanded the two men. "You both slipped on the rocks. Your weapon discharged accidentally," he said to the man who had fired a warning shot. "You never saw the girl or the boy. Return to your vehicle and seek medical attention."

Without a word, they turned and began working their way around the lake again, the one with the broken wrist groaning with every step, breath coming hard. As they moved away, Major reached down, picked up Wally's backpack, and threw it as far as he could out into the lake. It splashed into the water and sank without a trace.

He started around the lake after his men, checking his cell phone as he walked – carefully, he didn't want to fall again – and wasn't surprised to find there was no service. But once they were back on the main road, he would call his pilot.

They were heading to Regina.

◀◀ ▶▶

Ariane didn't have a destination in mind when she whisked Wally and the third shard away from the lake. She only wanted to get away. And she wanted to get Wally warm. He'd looked so cold, all-but-naked, blue and shivering, that she was afraid he was tipping into hypothermia.

I shouldn't even care what happens to him, she thought.

But she did.

So she headed back to Queenstown, to an indoor pool she sensed as they zipped that way through pipes and filters. It wasn't until they were already materializing that she realized this was about to get very awkward for both of them...but especially for Wally.

Even as she thought that, she thought, *Serves him right* – and then, suddenly they were in the swimming pool, the sting of chlorine in her eyes. She surfaced, spluttering, and looked around. They were in a huge open recreation area, crowded with people, mostly children in the pool they were in, adults in swimsuits sitting around the pool edges on white plastic chairs. There was a hot tub not far away, three men and four women basking in it. There was a weird yellow giant-mushroom thing spraying water in all directions, children screaming as they ran around in it. Light streamed in through big glass windows in the strangely slanted walls.

She hauled herself out of the water. She didn't dare order the water off herself with all those people around, so she spluttered and held out her hand for Wally. "Come on," she said. "We have go get out of here."

"I can't get out!" Wally protested. "I'm in my underwear!"

"You can't stay in the water either," Ariane said.

"At least get me a towel!"

"Fine." She turned away, took a step, and stopped. "Uh-oh."

A lifeguard, a girl just a little older than Ariane in a black one-piece bathing suit, was making her determined way toward them. "What are you doing in the pool in your clothes?" she cried. "You'll foul the filters!"

"Sorry," Ariane said. She tried what she hoped was a winning smile. "Fell in."

The girl pointed at her feet. "*And* you're wearing street shoes. I could have you banned from the pool for that!"

"Sorry," Ariane said again.

The girl gave her a closer look. "You're not from here," she said. "American?"

"Canadian."

"Well, even in Canada they should know better," the girl said with a sniff, and Ariane decided she didn't like her. "Now get out of here before I report you."

"My friend..." Ariane gestured at Wally, who was treading water with only his eyes showing above the surface.

"At least he's dressed for swimming," the girl said with

a glance. "You can wait for him in the viewing area." She pointed to big glass windows that overlooked the pool in the slanting wall above the yellow mushroom. "Go on."

Ariane gave Wally an apologetic look, though she was smirking inside. She meekly crossed the pool and found the stairs up to the second-floor viewing area. Halfway up, she wished herself dry, spraying the concrete walls with water. Once inside the viewing room, empty except for her, she sat in a comfortable chair, folded her arms, and waited to see what Wally would do.

He swam over to the edge of the pool and hung there for a long time, staring up at the viewing area. She waved at him.

Five minutes went by. She didn't move. He didn't move. And then, finally, convulsively, he hauled himself out of the water. Head down, arms wrapped around himself, dripping, undershorts sagging with water, he trudged along the verge of the pool, head down. Ariane saw people pointing at him and laughing. Even from where she sat she could see he was turning red. He grabbed a towel from a stack by the entrance and wrapped it around himself, then disappeared, presumably into the men's change area.

Ariane debated letting him just stew in there for a while, but in the back of her mind was the realization that Rex Major must be heading down from Lake Putahi by now. She didn't know what he would do, but she knew he'd never give up.

We need to make plans, she thought, getting to her feet and heading back down the stairs to the main floor. *We need to...*

She stopped at the bottom of the stairs, hand on the rail, staring at nothing.

We?

Wally Knight had betrayed her to Rex Major. Wally Knight had stolen the second shard from her and given it to Major...to Merlin. He had lied to her. He'd...

He just handed you the third shard, she reminded herself. *He rescued Aunt Phyllis.*

He told you he rescued Aunt Phyllis, she thought. *But he hasn't exactly given you reason to believe everything he says, has he? What if he's still helping Major? What if this is all some kind of plot of Major's?*

Some ridiculously overcomplicated and obtuse plot, she told herself. Because she would have handed Major the third shard without any fuss at all if Wally hadn't appeared on the island. She would probably have given him the first shard, too. There was no way *this* was helping Major. Which had to mean Wally had betrayed him just as he had betrayed her.

That still doesn't mean I can trust him.

But she couldn't leave him stranded in a New Zealand swimming pool dressing room with only his underwear, either. So she carried on down the stairs, around the corner, and down the hall to the entrance to the men's dressing room. She hesitated, looking around, then pushed the door open a crack and called, "Wally?"

There was a second door inside, on the other side of a kind of airlock to ensure privacy. She took another look up and down the hall. No one was in sight. She ducked into the space between the doors and opened the second one a little bit. "Wally?" she said again.

The door swung open. There he was, towel wrapped around his middle. She glimpsed someone else's pink flesh behind him and quickly turned away. "Come in here," she said.

He stepped into the "airlock" and let the door close behind him. "I don't have any clothes," he said. He sounded panicked. "Or money. Or a passport. Everything was in my backpack."

"I don't have any money either," Ariane said.

"What do we do?"

Ariane chewed on her lip, thinking. "Look, you're in the men's dressing room," she said at last. "Maybe you can find something?"

"Steal someone else's clothes?" Wally said.

"Well, at least anyone whose clothes you take *lives* here," Ariane pointed out. "They can call someone, get some clothes sent over. You don't have any options. Unless you like running around in your underwear."

Wally sighed. "All right. I'll see what I can do. Wait for me outside."

"I'm certainly not waiting for you in here!" Ariane said. Wally turned and went back inside, and Ariane stepped out through the other swinging door into the hallway...

...which was no longer empty. A tall black woman just emerging from the women's dressing room gave her a startled look as she popped out of the men's. "Brother," she babbled, feeling she had to say something. "Forgot his trunks. Just..." Her voice trailed off as the woman, shaking her head, moved on down the hall.

Ariane leaned against the wall and sighed. Then she dug in her pocket and pulled out the third shard of Excalibur. It sang to her, sorrowfully, it seemed, sad not to have been reunited with the second shard that had been so close.

But she could feel its power, and *that* was new. When she had had the first shard in her possession and Merlin had had the second, she had been unable to draw on the power of the shard she had. But she *knew* she could draw on this one's power.

It must be because of the first shard, she thought. *Even though I left it behind, this one knows I have it. The fact Merlin has one of them can't keep me from using this one.*

And there had been something else, too.

She almost thought she'd imagined it, but when Wally had handed her the shard, during that brief moment when they were both touching it, it had seemed to surge in power, as though its song had risen from *pianissimo* to *fortissimo* in a heartbeat. It was like when he had briefly held both shards in France, and the discordant song they made had suddenly melded into one glorious harmony.

What's Wally's connection to the sword? she wondered. *"Astonishing,"* the Lady had said when she'd seen Wally under Wascana Lake. *"Of course you would be drawn to me...I wonder if Merlin..."* Ariane had no idea what she'd meant by that. She doubted Wally did, either. But Major... Major probably knew *exactly* what Wally's connection with the sword was. He needed Wally for something, or he would never have bothered with the whole "come live with me in Toronto" charade.

But even so...

She had almost died crossing the Atlantic. The only way she could see to get home – especially since Major still had her newly minted passport – was to try to use the clouds. But the Pacific was far wider than the Atlantic. And not only that...

Not only that, she would have to take Wally with her.

I should just leave him here now, she thought. *I could take off right now.*

But he'd lost his clothes, his passport, his wallet, everything in his backpack, when she'd rushed them away from the lake. He'd be stranded indefinitely if she left him alone.

Serve him right, she thought sourly, but she still couldn't bring herself to do it.

And so she stood in the hallway outside the men's dressing room, and waited for Wally to emerge.

Despite everything he had done to her, it felt...right.

But she still had *one* little payback surprise in store for him.

CHAPTER FIFTEEN

THE RACE TO REGINA

WELL, this HAS BEEN THE MOST EMBARRASSING *day of my life*, Wally thought as he tried locker after locker in the men's change room. And considering how many embarrassing days he had had in his not-quite-fifteen years, that was saying something.

It got worse. Good news! He found an open locker. Bad news! The man it belonged to was clearly twice Wally's size. But at least what he had left in the locker was a pair of grey sweatpants – with some kind of animal paw print in bright green on the rear end, Wally saw with resignation – that had a drawstring he could pull as tight as he liked. He secured the waist, then rolled up the legs. The result made him look like a circus clown with no talent for costuming, but at least it covered him more-or-less respectably. The sweatshirt he also found, which was adorned with a purple-blue skull that featured a Union Jack around the right eyehole, four red stars in a diamond formation on the left side, and the enigmatic word *HANDSKULL* in capital letters underneath that, could actually have served as his *only* item of clothing, since it hung down within spitting distance of his knees. There were no shoes and he was sure there was no way he could have worn them if there had been. *Barefoot it is*, he thought, and with a furtive look around the almost-empty dressing room, half-expecting some naked giant of a rugby player to come roaring at him for stealing his clothes, darted for the door.

Ariane was waiting for him in the hall. She looked grim, but a half-smile still twitched across her face when she saw him. "Suits you," she said. The not-quite-a-smile faded. "Let's get out of here."

They walked out through the glassed-in lobby of the pool, Wally's odd get-up earning a doubletake from the teenage girl at the counter. *I've always* wanted *girls to give me a second look*, he thought sadly. *That's not quite how I imagined it.*

There was a big grassy park on the other side of the parking lot. They walked out into it. Wally twisted his head up to look as a jet came roaring in, seemingly at tree-top level at the end of the park, and he realized with a start that they were right next door to the Queenstown airport.

Which does me no good at all. He had no money, no passport, no clothes. It was all back at Lake Putahi.

"What do we do now?" Wally said. Ariane was walking silently ahead of him, trudging across the park as though she intended to walk all the way to Canada, which was roughly the direction she was headed.

"I'm not sure there is any 'we,'" Ariane said. She stopped at last, and turned back to Wally, fists clenching at her sides. *That's not a good sign*, he thought uneasily. He smiled tentatively at her. She didn't smile back. Instead, her fist came lashing out and caught him on the cheek, so hard he found himself on the ground on his hands and knees without quite knowing how he had ended up there, ears ringing and the taste of blood in his mouth. He raised a shaking hand to his face. "Ow," he said. "Now I know how Draco Malfoy felt when Hermione punched him." He tried to say it lightly, but in his heart he was terrified. Had he really broken things so badly with Ariane?

With the Lady of the Lake, he reminded himself. *She put your sister in the hospital. And she's got one of those shards in her pocket right now.*

He scrambled to his feet, took a couple of steps away just in case, and then turned to face Ariane, putting one hand to his bruised face. "Ow," he said again.

Ariane was grimacing and shaking her hand. "I think I hurt myself more than I hurt you," she said. "Ow."

"So are we even?"

"No, we're not even." Ariane sounded close to tears. "Wally, you can't imagine...when I realized you'd stolen the shard, taken it to Rex Major...*why did you do it?*"

"I told you, over Skype," Wally said. To his surprise, his voice was trembling. "I thought it was the best thing for you. I didn't like...what the shards were doing to you. What you did to Flish. Then you hurt me, in the cave."

"So you decided to hurt *me*?" Ariane cried. "Wally, I thought we were friends."

"We were...we are." *I hope*, Wally thought desperately. *Oh, I hope...* "Ariane, I see now how wrong I was. I just...I let Major into my head. He can't Command me, but I believed him anyway when he said he really wanted what was best for you and the world. I believed him... right up until he started lying to me. When I found out he'd kidnapped Aunt Phyllis. After that..." He felt his voice catch in his throat, and cleared it noisily. "After that, I felt like an idiot. I felt like a traitor. I felt as badly as you could possibly hope I would feel, Ariane. And I set out to make it right. I rescued Aunt Phyllis. I got here in time to tell you she was free so you could escape with the shard. I almost froze to death..."

"Next time pack a wetsuit," Ariane said. She was

blinking hard. "Wally...I *want* to believe you. I want you back as a friend. I want your help in this quest. The Lady gave it to both of us. It didn't go well in France when I tried to do it myself. I *need* you. But I have to know I can trust you."

"You can," Wally said. "Ariane, I promise. I was an idiot. I won't be taken in again."

Ariane looked down at the ground. When she looked up again, her eyes were shining. "All right, Wally," she said. "I believe you. And I forgive you."

Wally wanted to hug her. Actually, he wanted to kiss her. But that seemed a little too much too soon, so instead he just folded his arms over the ugly sweatshirt and mumbled, "So, what now?" He glanced over his shoulder. "I can't fly out without my passport, and it's at the lake. So is my backpack. And my real clothes." He looked down at his ridiculous getup, and sighed. "They wouldn't let me on an airplane looking like this anyway."

Ariane chewed on your lip. "An airplane will be too slow," she said. "There may be another way."

Wally blinked. "What?"

Ariane dug in her pocket for the third shard. She held it out. "Touch it," she said.

Wally reached out a finger. Again, as he had on the island, he felt...something. He couldn't quite say what. A feeling. A sensation. A hot flash, maybe. He jerked his finger back.

Ariane had obviously felt more. She smiled a real smile for the first time since she'd seen him on the island. "I don't think you're going to need an airplane, Wally," she said. "But let's go get your backpack just the same...if it's still there."

He blinked. "What...?"

She held out the shard again, this time with her fist around one end. "Take hold of this," she said. "And don't let go. But don't grip too tightly. It's still pretty sharp."

Gingerly, he took hold of the end she'd offered him. "I don't under…" The word would have ended in squeak… if he had still had vocal chords.

One instant they were standing in the grass of the park. The next they were rushing upward, and…expanding. He felt huge, enormously huge, as big as…

…as big as a cloud!

This is how Ariane got to France, he thought, though how he could be thinking anything without his head he had no idea. *She said she couldn't do this with me!*

Just for an instant he wondered if she were so furious, and so Lady-like, that she intended to kill him, letting him drift away, dematerialized, or worse, materializing him at ten thousand feet and letting him fall. But he shoved that doubt away. If he wanted Ariane to trust him, he had to trust her.

The strange thing was, as they rushed through the clouds toward the mountains that towered over Queenstown, he could still feel his hand clutching the shard of Excalibur, hard and sharp and present, even though it was as invisible and immaterial as his own body. He even knew he could let go of it if he chose. He thought that was probably a really, really bad idea, though. Instead he clutched it tighter, and actually felt pain as the sharp edge cut into his flesh.

That makes no sense, he thought. *Where are our bodies really?*

Then suddenly their bodies "really" were with their minds again, as they materialized in Lake Putahi and waded ashore. Wally released the shard and looked at the thin line of red on the ball of his thumb. Ariane wished them dry while Wally took a nervous look around, half-expecting Rex Major and his men to still be there. But there was no one.

There was no sign of his backpack, either. He groaned. "Major must have taken it."

Ariane knelt down and put her hand in the water. She closed her eyes for a second. "No," she said. "No…it's still here. Just give me a second." She waded back into the lake.

Wally looked at the shallow half-inch cut where he had gripped the shard too tightly while still in the cloud. It stung. He sucked at it as he watched Ariane disappear in a swirl of disturbed water. Twenty seconds went by… thirty…and then she reappeared in a fountain of spray. She waded out again, his backpack clutched in her hand. Water sprayed out from her and the backpack. When she handed it to Wally, it was bone dry. He pulled out his own clothes. "Turn your back," he told Ariane.

"I've already seen you in your underwear, you know," Ariane said sweetly. "So have half the kids in Queenstown, back at the pool."

Wally blushed. "Turn your back anyway," he said.

Ariane smirked and turned her back. Wally got dressed as quickly as he could. "All right," he said after he'd zipped up his jeans. When Ariane turned around he was pulling on his socks and shoes. "That's better," he said with relief, and stood. He put his hand on his hips. "Now tell me…how did you do that? You said you couldn't travel through the clouds with me!"

Ariane shrugged. "I couldn't…until you were touching the shard, too. I don't know why, but that gives it way more power than when I'm holding it all by myself." She looked up at the clouds. "I think…I think I can get both of us all the way back to Regina through the clouds. Without running out of steam like I did crossing the Atlantic."

"Like you…" Wally felt a chill. "What?"

Ariane gave him a steady look. "I couldn't use the first shard's power while we had only uncovered two of them and Rex Major had the other," she said. "I reached for it, and it wasn't there. If I hadn't found a cruise ship to materialize on, I would have died."

Wally felt sick. "Ariane...I didn't know...I never would have..." He closed his eyes and hung his head. "I was such an idiot."

"Like you said, you didn't know," Ariane said.

"I could have killed you."

Ariane shook her head. "*Rex Major* could have killed me. And I think he would have been fine with that." She took a deep breath. "You've got money now?"

Wally nodded.

"Then let's go back to town and get something to eat. I need to be fuelled up if we're going to do this."

"Major is probably already at the airport," Wally pointed out.

"It's not a race," Ariane said. "He doesn't know where the first shard is." She frowned. "But I'd still like to get back before him. Because if he starts looking hard enough, he'll find Aunt Phyllis again. I've got to reach her before he does. Better make it fast food." She reached out her hand to Wally. "We won't take the clouds this time."

"Not the swimming pool again," he groaned.

Ariane laughed. "No," she said. "We'll find something else."

Wally took her hand. She led him into the water, and let it suck them down and away.

◄◄ ►►

Ariane sat across from Wally eating a foot-long submarine sandwich. Normally she only ordered a six-inch one, but she needed all the calories she could get before they attempted the flight to Regina.

Wally's cheek was purpling where she'd slugged him

and her knuckles still hurt. *That whole punching people in the face thing looks way easier on TV than it is in real life*, she thought. She shouldn't have done it – but it had felt good.

And that little bit of violence hadn't been coming from the sword, either.

She'd told Wally she'd trust him. She *wanted* to trust him. But there was still a tiny seed of doubt as she looked at him: residual damage from the hurt he had caused her when he'd betrayed her to Rex Major. She hoped it would heal with time. He looked the same as always…ears too big, face freckled, red hair and a rather alarming grin. He still wasn't handsome. But she didn't think he was homely anymore either. He was just…Wally.

It felt good to have him back at her side. It really did.

But that little thread of doubt still lingered.

He finished his sandwich, tilted his bag of chips to shake out the last few bits, slurped down the last of his Coke, burped, said "Excuse me," a little shamefacedly, and then wiped his face with his napkin. "All set," he said.

She realized she'd been staring at him instead of eating. She hastily downed the rest of her own meal, then stood up. "No time like the present," she said.

The sandwich shop was only a block from Lake Wakatipu. They walked back to the same place where they'd materialized when they'd arrived from Lake Putahi. Wally had pointed out they could have just used the big lake the first time instead of popping up in a swimming pool. Ariane had sweetly pointed out that showing up in his underwear downtown would have been way more embarrassing than showing up in the pool had been, and he'd had to admit she had a point. A low stone wall separated the lakeshore from the street, but an opening not far off led down onto the beach. There were other people down there, but they were some distance away. Ariane took out the shard and held it out to Wally. "Here we go."

He looked a little pale – she couldn't blame him for that – but he reached out and grasped the other end of the shard firmly, even though his hand was bandaged from the previous trip. *I told him not to grip too tightly*, she thought, but she couldn't really blame him for that, either.

Just as before, she felt an enormous surge of power in the shard when Wally had hold of it with her. It was almost as though the sword belonged as much to him as to her, but that made no sense. *She* was the Lady of the Lake, and he was just a kid who'd happened to be on the shore when she'd first heard the Lady's song.

Except, clearly, he was more than that. But how that could be, she had no idea.

All that mattered, though, was the power: power enough to keep both of them aloft long enough, she hoped, to make it across the Pacific.

There was no possibility of taking a direct route. She had to leap from cloud to cloud when they were scattered, though she could race in a straight line through overcast skies. She could hear in her mind, distant but clear, the song of the first shard she had claimed for herself, nestled in its hiding place, and she used that as her compass.

Time had no meaning. Everything narrowed down to the journey, the steady flow of power from the shard into her. She knew Wally was with her, but they could not speak in any fashion. She just hoped he didn't let go of the shard. If he did, she didn't think she could save him.

But even that fear seemed remote. When she was using the power of the sword, everyday human concerns grew distant. There was always – *always* – the urge in the back of her mind to simply let herself go into the clouds, let her mind dissolve with her body, become one with the water. She wouldn't give into it. She'd already fought and won that battle. But it was there, and if someday things changed, or things became so desperately bad in her life she could not endure it, she could always...

She caught herself. The magic's self-destructive urge was insidious. Even as she was thinking she'd resisted it, it had snaked its way into her mind.

It was a sign she was getting tired, her will weakening. The power of the shard seemed as strong as ever, but her ability to use it was fading. For the first time in a long time she tried to take stock of what lay beneath them.

She could tell it was dark, and with her own eyes she would surely have been blind, but somehow the magic let her see, or at least sense, what lay beneath them. There was ice in the ocean. How far north had they come? There was no fresh water down there to materialize in. But ahead...she could sense something...

Land. A town. A pool.

Good enough.

Thirty seconds later they emerged, spluttering, in an empty, darkened swimming pool. The glow from a few blue nightlights revealed high walls, steel beams holding up a metal roof. There were windows high up in one wall, but only a hint of reflected streetlight came through them.

They hauled themselves out onto the pool verge and Ariane dried them. "Where are we?" Wally said.

"Kvimarvik Swimming Pool," Ariane said.

Wally blinked. "How do you know?"

She pointed over his head. He twisted around and saw the name on the wall. "Oh." He twisted around again. "And where is that?"

"Either Alaska or B.C., I think," Ariane said. She heaved a sigh. She felt exhausted. "I have to rest before we go on. Food would be good, too."

"Your wish is my command," Wally said. He dug in his backpack and hauled out a handful of granola bars.

"Courtesy of Rex Major. I stole them from his condo kitchen before I escaped."

Ariane took them eagerly. After the first one she felt much better. After four she thought she could almost manage to get them moving again. But she still needed a few more minutes' rest. She told Wally.

"Suits me," he said. He shuddered. "That is *not* a nice way to travel as a passenger. Give me a business-class seat in a 747 any day."

"Hey, I could have left you in New Zealand," Ariane said, feeling obscurely stung. "It's not that bad."

"Maybe not for you," Wally said. "You're driving. I was just...there and not there." He shook his head. "I don't think I like magic."

"Magic likes *you*," Ariane said. "It's only because you're holding the other end of the shard I have enough power to move us both. What's that all about, anyway?"

Wally sighed. "I really have no idea." He hesitated. "But I can...sense...the shard, too. Probably not as strongly as you can, but when I got to Lake Putahi...I knew it was on the island."

"You've definitely got some connection to the sword," Ariane said. "I just wish I knew what it was."

"You and me both," Wally said. "Merlin kept telling me there was something special about me, that my involvement in all this isn't an accident. But he never explained. Doesn't seem likely he's going to now."

Ariane laughed a little. "Probably not." She stretched, and stood up. "All right," she said. "Let's keep going."

Wally groaned, but stood. "Can't see the clouds from in here."

"We'll take the waterways," Ariane said. "As far as we can, anyway." She frowned. "I wonder where Major is."

"Assuming this is the same day – or the day before, I can never remember how the International Date Line works – we left New Zealand, he should still be flying, shouldn't he? How long did it take you?"

"Maybe...eleven or twelve hours in the air. But he'll have to stop to refuel. And that was from Vancouver. If he's heading to Saskatchewan it'll be another three hours or so on top of that. He shouldn't be there yet. Anyway, like I said, it shouldn't matter. He doesn't know where the shard is."

"You keep saying that," Wally said darkly. "But I wouldn't want to bet money on it."

Uneasily, Ariane realized he was right. What if Major had some way to find the first shard? What if her having the third one didn't block his use of the second, and he could hear it singing?

"Let's get moving," she said.

They plunged into the pool and away through the pipes. She kept to streams and rivers and lakes as much as she could, though twice she leaped them up to the clouds and down again when that seemed more direct.

Again, she didn't know how long it took, but suddenly they were there, in Wascana Lake, in the dark. She materialized them and they clambered out through a thin skein of ice onto the shore: right at the place where it had all begun, at the foot of the parking lot at the lake's northeast corner. She dried them. The song of the sword sang to her. "Wait here," she said to Wally. "I'll be back in a flash."

She stepped back in the water, became one with it. Her senses expanded. Now that she wasn't travelling, she could use her power in another way, the same way she had used it back at Lake Putahi to find Wally's backpack. She could sense everything in the lake: every grocery cart, every beer bottle, every strange object that had made its way into Wascana since the Big Dig that had deepened the lake when she was little. But none of those mattered. What mattered was the joyful song of the first shard of

Excalibur, the one she had held the longest. In all the muddy detritus at the bottom of the lake, it stood out in her mind like a shining diamond...no, more than that, a star, a point of pure white fire.

She gathered it to herself, returned to her body, rose dripping and triumphant from the water at the foot of the parking lot with the shard in her hand...

And stopped dead.

Wally was where she had left him, but he wasn't alone. A man, a fat man, breathing hard, had an arm around Wally's chest, pinning his arms to his side. The man's other hand held a knife, just pricking the skin below Wally's right ear. Ariane saw a streak of dark blood running down Wally's neck.

"I'll take that," the man panted.

CHAPTER SIXTEEN

A KNIFE TO THE THROAT

WALLY STOOD IN THE COLD, arms wrapped around himself, breath coming in clouds lit white by the lights of the empty parking lot behind him. He wondered what time it was. The city was never entirely silent, but the traffic noise was as little as he'd ever heard it. 3 a.m.? 4 a.m.? Whichever, the park was deserted.

Ariane had simply vanished. He half-expected her to emerge on Willow Island, but there was no sign of her anywhere. He sighed and stamped his feet. Maybe he could spend the night in his own bed. That would make a nice change.

And then, with no warning at all, someone grabbed him from behind. Shocked, he didn't even struggle as an enormous flabby arm wrapped around him, and then it was too late. Something cold touched his neck below his right ear, then stung. Warmth dribbled down his neck.

"What –" he said...or squeaked, really.

"Shut up," said a man's voice. "Or I stick the knife in farther."

Wally shut up.

As suddenly as she had vanished, Ariane returned. She

appeared in the water in an explosion of spray, got her feet under her, started to wade ashore...and froze when she saw Wally and his captor in front of her.

"I'll take that," said the man.

The water behind Ariane swirled and began to rise up into tentacles, and the man's grip on Wally tightened. "None of that," he growled. "Mr. Major told me about your tricks. I see anything coming out of that lake besides you, your boyfriend loses an ear."

"If you kill him, I'll kill you," Ariane said in a voice so cold it made Wally's eyes widen in surprise.

"Who said anything about killing him?" the man said. Wally could feel the man's heart pounding in his chest, hear his breath coming in gasps. *He's scared*, Wally thought. But it didn't seem to be stopping him. "I can cut him up plenty without killing him. How long are you willing to watch that before you give me the shard?"

"How do you know about the shard?" Wally gasped. "Who are you?"

The grip never slackened. "Anderson Bukowski. District sales manager, Excalibur Computer Systems."

Wally groaned. What was it with Rex Major and his district sales managers? He'd Commanded the last one to try to kidnap Ariane before they'd even found the first shard. *They're like Hogwarts's Defense Against the Dark Arts instructors*, he thought.

"Let him go," Ariane said. "Why are you doing this?"

"Because Mr. Major told me to," Bukowski said.

"He told you to attack a fourteen-year-old kid?"

"He told me to watch Willow Island," he said. "He told me if you showed up, to stop you from getting the shard of Excalibur you hid in the lake. He told me what you could do with water and told me to be creative if I had to try to stop you." He jerked Wally back against himself, hard. "I'm being creative."

Ariane stood frozen, indecisive. *I guess she's almost decided she can trust me,* he thought. *Otherwise she'd already be gone. That's a good thing.*

But nothing else about the situation was good. It was the opposite of good.

More than that, it was infuriating.

The anger rising in Wally seemed to be coming from outside himself, flowing to him from some other source. It only took him a second to realize what that meant.

The sword was calling to him. Excalibur was...speaking? singing?...he couldn't quite describe what it felt like, but one thing he knew. The sword knew him. The sword wanted to help him. The sword was giving him power just as it gave Ariane power.

But not the same kind of power. Mostly, it was filling him up with anger – and a sudden confidence that the bumbling, overweight, would-be murderous, district sales manager holding him was no match for what he could do.

What can *I do?*

This.

He let the power singing in him take over. He stomped down on Bukowski's foot. Bukowski swore, his grip loosened, and that was all Wally needed. He twisted, down and out from under the big arm, spun around and with a roundhouse kick knocked Bukowski's feet out from under him. Bukowski thudded to the ground, breath *whooshing!* out of him, arms flung wide. The knife skittered across the pavement. Wally leaped on it, spun, planted his knee on the man's chest, pulled back the knife to drive it into Bukowski's throat...

And then a tentacle of water slapped across his ribs and sent him tumbling away from the district sales manager, whose face was purpling as he struggled to breathe. Spluttering, enraged, Wally got to his feet, turned back, knife still in his hand, ready to attack Bukowski once more...

and suddenly realized what he was doing. He dropped the blade in horror.

I was going to kill him, he thought. *I would* have killed *him if Ariane hadn't stopped me. I've never wanted to kill anyone in my life!* He looked down at his hands as if they belonged to a stranger. *How did I do that? Why* did I do *that?*

The sword. Now he understood how Ariane could have hurt his sister so badly. He understood how much effort it had taken her not to hurt his sister worse.

Whatever his connection to Excalibur was, the connection Merlin would not tell him about, it was as a warrior.

Wally the Warrior.

Once the thought that he might actually be a warrior, a knight in more than surname, would have excited him. But remembering that moment when he had planted his knee in Bukowski's chest and been fully prepared to drive the dagger into the man's throat, he felt only terror.

Excalibur was in pieces yet it was already making its power felt. What would it be like when it was whole?

One thing was certain. They couldn't let Major have it. What *he* would do with that power…

"Wally!" Ariane cried. "Hurry up! Let's get out of here."

Wally realized he'd been simply standing, staring at his hands, which had started to tremble. He clenched them into fists and ran over to Ariane. She grabbed his arm, they stepped into the water, and then they were gone.

◀ ▶

Rex Major was still in the air, an hour short of Regina, when the call came in. Anderson Bukowski, the only man he'd had available for the job, had lost the first shard. Somehow, though Major would have sworn it was impossible, Ariane had made it back to Regina ahead of him.

Not only that, she'd managed to bring Wally with her.

Major, furious, came within a heartbeat of Commanding Bukowski to drown himself in the lake from which he'd let Ariane escape. But he'd drawn quite enough attention to Excalibur Computer Systems in Regina already, what with his last district sales manager having been arrested for climbing into the bedroom of a teenage girl. So he reined in his temper and instead Commanded Bukowski to forget everything he'd seen and been told to do. Any lingering memory he would dismiss as a dream, for he would immediately go home and go to bed.

That done, Major leaned back in his chair, steepled his fingers, and brooded.

Ariane's feat could only mean one thing: now that she had two shards, the fact he still held one was not blocking her use of at least one of them. Though he still didn't understand how she'd managed to apparently use *both* of them.

Unless…

He sighed. He'd wanted absolute proof that Wally carried the blood of Arthur in his veins. Apparently he had it. The sword had recognized the connection. It had provided Wally with the skill and strength he needed to defeat Bukowski.

The blood of Arthur in his veins. Major shook his head. That was the way they would have talked about it back when Arthur still walked the Earth. These days they would more likely talk about "genes." But the truth was: it had nothing to do with either blood or genes. It was magic. This many centuries down the line from Arthur, his genetic material would be spread among thousands of descendants. But only to *this* family, in this time, had the magic attached itself, just as the Lady's magic had attached itself to Ariane's line.

This family…

Wally had a sister.

Not only that, Wally had a sister whom Ariane had already made into an enemy. In fact, from what Wally had told him, she was still in the hospital recovering from the injuries Ariane had inflicted. Maybe, just maybe, he didn't need Wally.

They'd be on the ground in an hour. The computer on the airplane had a satellite Internet connection. He did a quick Google search. Regular visiting hours at the Regina General Hospital began at 11 a.m. He'd have a quick nap when they got in, then attack the problem from a fresh new angle.

The fourth shard will be revealing itself soon, he thought. *I won't be thwarted again. Ariane can be manipulated through hostages. I've proved that more than once. I just need a better hostage.*

He doubted Ariane would let him get hold of Aunt Phyllis again. She'd be tucked away somewhere his magic wouldn't reach. Fortunately, he had an ace up his sleeve Ariane knew nothing about.

He activated his remote access to his home computer back in Toronto, and opened the file folder he remembered. There was the photo from the Carlyle convenience store. Emily Forsythe. Ariane's mother. Ever since that first contact, he'd had someone looking for her, and all his computer feelers extended. The computers had turned up nothing: she was doing an excellent job of staying off the grid. But just a few days ago there *had* been a new development from his man – woman, in this case – on the ground. She had a lead. A woman answering Emily Forsythe's description had been admitted to hospital in Yorkton. Major had already dispatched his operative to check it out.

If Ariane's mother were still alive – and if he could get to her – then every attempt Ariane had made to keep the shards from him would come to naught. He knew the girl well enough now to know she would give up everything to keep her mother safe, even if she had all the shards – even with the sword screaming in her ear, as he knew it would, to serve its needs instead of her own.

He could still win this battle. He could still win even if he didn't find Ariane's mother, if he could find the fourth shard before she did.

He fingered the ruby stud in his ear. Once all four pieces of the blade had been found, he was certain the final piece, the hilt, would also make itself known. With it, and two of the other shards, he could bend the sword to his will. In that scenario, the shards themselves would force Ariane to give them up.

But he'd rather convince Ariane to just hand them over. It would be simpler, and cleaner. He didn't *want* to hurt anyone he didn't have to. But he *would* hurt anyone he did.

The pilot came onto the intercom, warning him that they were beginning their descent into Regina. *First things first,* he thought. *Let's see if Felicia Knight shares more with her little brother than a last name.*

◀▶

Ariane didn't go far: just the length of the lake to the Knight swimming pool. It felt almost like home, emerging there. For Wally, of course, it *was* home. She dried them both off, and then he led her to the kitchen. "I'm starving," he said. "And exhausted. But starving more. Want something to eat?" He opened the refrigerator's freezer compartment. "There are some microwave pizzas. Good enough?"

"Anything," Ariane said. She hadn't realized until that moment just how hungry she was, after using her power so hard and for so long. The granola bars in Alaska or wherever they'd been now seemed ancient history. She watched Wally pull out the pizzas and pop them in the microwave. As the machine whirred, she said, "Wally, how did you do that?"

"Do what?" he said, without turning around.

"You know what. You took that man down like a martial-arts expert or something. You never told me anything about taking self-defence classes."

Wally kept staring at the rotating pizzas in the microwave. "It wasn't me," he said in a low voice. "It was the sword."

Ariane blinked. "What?"

Now he turned around. "The sword," he said. "I can feel it too, Ariane. I don't know if it's what you feel. I certainly can't travel through water. But I can feel it. It's... after me."

She raised an eyebrow. "*After* you?"

"It wants me. It wants me to...wield it, I guess. And it's...feeding me. Ability I shouldn't have." He sighed. "I noticed it in fencing class: suddenly I was one of the best fencers on the team, when before...I wasn't. Then when I was escaping from Rex Major...I almost killed the guard there by hitting him with a poker. I didn't intend to hit him at all. Just..."

"Poke him?" Ariane said.

He made a face. "It wasn't funny. There was blood everywhere. And now, tonight..." He shook his head. "I not only took that guy down, I was two seconds from killing him. If you hadn't stopped me..."

Ariane knew well enough the call of the sword to kill her enemies. She knew why *she* felt it: she was the heir to the power of the Lady of the Lake, who had made the sword, or caused it to be made, and put into it whatever power it had. But why was Wally feeling it? Why, when he touched the shard, did it suddenly become more powerful? Why had he been able to join two shards together in perfect harmony when she couldn't?

She had two shards now, but they couldn't be joined together: the first shard was the point, the third shard was from somewhere halfway up the blade. But she could feel that their songs were ever so slightly out of tune with each other.

She pulled them both out and held them out to Wally. "Hold these for a minute."

He drew back. "I don't –"

"Just for a second."

"I'm surprised you'd let me," Wally said. "After France."

"I think you just convinced me beyond a shadow of a doubt you're not working for Major," she said dryly, "since you just about skewered his district sales manager." She wriggled the two pieces of the sword at him. "Go on, hold them."

Hesitantly, as the microwave beeped behind him to announce the successful heating of the pizzas, he took hold of the two shards.

Instantly that faint, grating discord vanished. As the first and second had in France, so now the first and third sang together in perfect harmony.

Wally had a far-away look in his eye. "I can...almost... hear? I guess?...something..."

Ariane took the shards back. The discord returned, harder to take in the wake of that beautiful song. She tucked both shards into the pockets of her jeans. "You've definitely got a connection to the sword," she said. "I wish I knew why, or what it means."

"You and me both," Wally said. He turned around and pulled out the pizzas, and they sat at the kitchen counter and ate them. They tasted pretty much the way cardboard smeared with melted cheese probably tasted, and she thought she'd never eaten anything more wonderful in her life.

They washed down the pizzas with ginger ale, and then, all at once, Ariane's exhaustion really hit her. "I need bed," she said, yawning hugely.

"Me, too," Wally said. "You can have Flish's old room."

They plodded up the stairs. Wally put his hand on the handle of his room's door, and as it swung open, Ariane suddenly remembered what she had done to his room when she'd been in it a few days earlier. "Wally –" she began, but it was too late: he was gazing, aghast, at the torn posters and scattered books and clothes. "Um... sorry," she said. "I was...upset."

"No kidding," Wally said. He sighed. "Well, I deserved it." He rubbed his bruised face. "And more." Then he gave her a crooked grin. "Any more punishment to come, or are we good?"

"We're good," Ariane said. And then, moved by some strange impulse, she pulled him to her and hugged him tight. He went stiff for a moment, then returned the hug. "Wally, I'm glad we're friends again. I missed you."

"I missed you, too," he said, his voice muffled by her shoulder.

She let him go, stepped back. "Good night," she said, and went down the hallway. She still hated the purple décor in Flish's room. But the bed looked wonderful. She stripped off her clothes, climbed beneath the covers, and fell instantly asleep.

⬩⬩ ⬩⬩

Two doors down, Wally likewise undressed and climbed into bed, still feeling warm from the hug Ariane had given him, still feeling shaken by what had happened at the lake – and still hearing, distantly, the song of the two shards of Excalibur currently under his roof.

What do we do now? he wondered, and had no answer. He might have some mystical connection to the sword, but Ariane was the freaking Lady of the Lake, and that made her the leader of the quest. He suspected, though, they'd next be taking a watery trip down to Estevan to retrieve Aunt Phyllis. Ariane was right: Rex Major would soon figure out where she'd gone. They couldn't afford any more hostage-taking. Where they'd go after that, he hadn't a clue.

But before they took up the quest again, there was one thing he had to do: visit his sister in the hospital. They might not be close anymore, but she was still family. *Maybe a few days laid up after attacking Ariane has softened her*, he thought, but without much hope.

He'd float that idea with Ariane in the morning. *It's not like she'd have to come with me*, he reasoned.

That decided, his mind was free to worry the other matter like a dog with a bone. Who, or what, was he? The sword had given him great fighting prowess, made him stronger and faster, more skilled and more ruthless. It was as if it were channeling the spirit of some great warrior, focusing it on him...

Great warrior. Excalibur? The only great warrior who had ever wielded Excalibur had been King Arthur himself.

Could that be it? he wondered. *Does the sword think I'm Arthur? Or think it can make me into Arthur?*

And since when did the notion of inanimate objects "thinking" become something I could think without giving it a second thought?

Am I the modern equivalent of Arthur, like Ariane is the equivalent of the Lady of the Lake?

Except she isn't just "the equivalent," she really is *the*

Lady of the Lake: the Lady's heir.

Does that mean…does that mean I'm Arthur's heir?

The thought was so exciting it brought him upright in bed. He jumped up, remembered at the last second he wasn't wearing any clothes, grabbed a dressing gown and ran down to Ariane's room. He opened the door a crack. "Ariane!" he whispered. "Are you awake?"

"Mmmph?" He heard her roll over in bed. "What… Wally? I was asleep…is something wrong?" Her voice suddenly became more awake. "Is it Rex Major?"

"No, it's me. Can I come in?"

"Sure…"

He opened the door and went into Flish's room. There was enough light from the street outside to show him Ariane stretched out under the covers, which she'd pulled up to her chin. He sat on the bed beside her. "I think I know why I have a connection to the sword," Wally said. "I think…Ariane, I think I'm Arthur's heir!"

"King Arthur?"

Wally laughed. "No, Arthur the cartoon aardvark. Of course, King Arthur!" In a rush, he told her why he thought that made sense.

When he ran down, she was silent for a moment. Then, "You could be right," she said. "That would explain why the shards react to you the way they do."

"And that would explain why Rex Major was interested in me," Wally said. It stung to say it, but it was the truth. "It has nothing to do with me at all. Not *me* me. He wants a new Arthur under his wing. He wants someone to lead his army. I don't know what he can do with his magic once Excalibur is intact, but as a fencer, I can tell you one thing about swords: someone has to wield them."

"Then losing you may be as crippling to his plans as losing the sword," Ariane said. She sounded excited. "Wally, that's great!"

"Yeah!" he said...except right then he remembered the moment when he'd been ready to stick a knife in Bukowski's throat, and it wasn't so great after all. "But it's scary," he said in a small voice. "The sword almost took me over in the parking lot, made me do something terrible. And the more shards we find, the stronger it's going to get. What if next time you can't stop me...and I can't stop myself?"

"You can fight it, Wally," Ariane said. "I have to fight it, too. It wants both of us to use it as the weapon it was intended to be. But it's Major – Merlin – who wants a weapon. We don't need a weapon. We just need to keep it out of his hands."

"How?" Wally said. "If we succeed, and we get the whole sword...we're still stuck with the sword and he's still one of the richest men in the world. Sooner or later he'll get it from us."

"I don't know," Ariane said. "The Lady didn't tell us that little detail." She sighed. "Wally, can we talk about this in the morning? I can barely keep my eyes open."

"Sure," Wally said. He got up. "In the morning. Good night."

Ariane had already rolled onto her side, the top of the bedspread slipping down to reveal one bare white shoulder. "G'night," she said.

Wally swallowed. It wasn't the sword urging him to kiss that shoulder. That was all Wally.

Glad to know I'm still me, he said. *For the moment, at least.*

He went out, closed the door behind him, and went back to his own bed.

CHAPTER SEVENTEEN

VISITING HOURS

PROMPTLY AT 11 A.M., Rex Major walked into Felicia Knight's private hospital room. The teenager lay propped up in her bed, one cast-covered leg raised high by a complicated pulley system, reading something on an iPad. "Hello, Felicia," Major said calmly. He knew Wally called her Flish. He also knew she hated that.

Flish lowered the iPad. Her eyes widened. "You're –"

"Rex Major, yes," Major said. He walked to the side of her bed. "How are you feeling?"

"How do you think?" she said. There were fading bruises on her face. Then she grimaced. "Sorry. Don't mean to be rude." She looked past him. "Is Wally with you? Mom told me he was staying with you, last time she called. I didn't believe her, but if you're here –"

"Wally is…elsewhere," Major said. He sighed. "I'm afraid your brother was a disappointment."

"Yeah, he's good at that," Flish said. "What did he do?"

"Ran away," Major said. "I don't know where he is now."

Flish's eyes widened. "Ran away? Is he…safe?"

"As far as I know. He's with that Forsythe girl and

her aunt."

"He ran away to be with that...bitch?" Flish spat the insult as if it burned her mouth.

"I'm afraid so. But that's why I've come to you."

Flish blinked. "I don't follow."

"Can I show you something?"

Now she looked suspicious. "What?"

Major reached inside his jacket and took out the second shard of Excalibur. Flish's eyes widened again. "Cool," she breathed, and that reaction alone told Major volumes. "Can I hold it?"

"Please," he said. He held it out. "But be careful, it's sharp."

Merlin had not had a hand in the making of the sword. That had been all his sister's doing, back when they both shared a vision of what they wanted to accomplish in this world. But he was attuned to all magic, and the sword drew magic to itself through the tiny opening still left between this world and his. He could feel that magic every time he handled the shard, though he had not yet been able to draw on it because Ariane's possession of the other shards prevented him.

All that changed the moment Flish touched the shard while he still had hold of the other end. The power of the shard flared in his awareness like a searchlight being switched on, blinding in its intensity. He gasped a little and let go of it, and the sensation faded.

"It's really old," Flish said, turning it over and over. "And it feels...tingly. Weird." He held out his hand for her to give it back and, though it was just for a moment, he saw her hesitate, reluctant to let it go. But then she handed it back, and once again, as they both had hold of it, he felt that surge of power.

This was better than he'd hoped – far better. He hadn't noticed any such effect on the shard when Wally had first handed it over to him, but then he had been so eager to receive the shard he'd snatched it from the boy's hand. There'd only been a fraction of a second when their touches had overlapped.

The sword can only serve one master, he thought. *But who is the* true *master of the sword? The heir of the Lady of the Lake – or one of the heirs of Arthur?*

One thing he now knew for certain: the blood of Arthur, the strain of magic peculiar to that great King, ran in Felicia Knight as surely as it did in Wally. Though not in their parents: he could Command either of the senior Knights as easily as anyone else – and had, over the phone, to get their permission to offer what he said next, and to assure them they had no reason to worry about Wally or even to try to find out where he was.

"I've spoken to your parents," Major said. "I'd like to offer you the place in my household Wally had. I'd like you to come to Toronto. You're in your last year of high school. You can finish with a private tutor and start work for me at once. There'll be a very generous salary and other perks."

Flish gave him a searching look. "You *know* how creepy that sounds," she said. "What 'perks' are you talking about? And are they perks for me...or perks for *you*?"

Major shook his head. "I'm not talking about that sort of arrangement," he said, though he approved of her suspicion. If she were going to take the place he had thought Wally would have at the head of his armies, Excalibur in hand, she would need to cultivate cunning and suspicion and deviousness. From what he knew of her, she was already well along the path.

Arthur had had a half-sister, Morgan le Fay. Sometimes an ally, sometimes an enemy. They had reconciled at the end, and she had been one of those who had borne Arthur's body to the mysterious island of Avalon –

in reality, a portal to Faerie, still wide open (though heavily guarded) in those days. Merlin had hoped to find enough power in that place for him to heal the dying king, but Arthur's injuries had been too severe even for *his* magic. Arthur had died, and despite the legend, he would not be returning.

Except in the person of one of his two heirs: a brother and sister. *Odd how magic causes history to, if not exactly repeat itself, then to echo itself down through the ages*, Merlin thought.

He regarded Flish. *I wasn't able to save Arthur*, he thought. *But maybe, with the power of the shard…*

"Let me show you something else," Major said. He held out the shard. "Touch this again, but don't take it from me."

Frowning, Flish did so. Again Major felt the surge of power. It didn't come close to equalling what he had once had, but it was as much greater than the little he had managed to hold onto as a bonfire was to a match. He closed his eyes, reached out his right hand, and touched Flish's cast-covered leg. The bones were aligned: the doctors had seen to that. It was a simple matter of convincing them to return to their accustomed, unbroken state. A little surge of magic and…

Flish gasped, and snatched her hand away from the shard. "What…what did you just…?"

Major turned and regarded the cast. The power was fading, but he had enough to…

He touched the hard plaster. With a loud crack, it broke in two and fell away, leaving Flish's leg bare…and whole.

Flish gasped again. "What are you doing? You can't –"

"Your leg is fine," Major said. "I just healed it. With magic."

"You're crazy!" Flish said.

"Am I? Does your leg still ache?"

"No..."

"Can you bend it?"

Flish tried. Her face went slack with amazement, then a fierce delight. "Wow!" she said. "Oh, wow!"

She swung the leg over the side of the bed. She stood up, swayed, and clutched at Rex Major. She grinned at him. And then she looked past him and her grin grew wider...and meaner.

He turned. Wally Knight and Ariane Forsythe stood in the hospital doorway. He smiled. "Hello, Wally, Ariane. Nice of you to visit."

◂◂ ▸▸

Wally had slept late. So had Ariane. It was almost 11 a.m. before they even left the house, and it took them twenty minutes to walk to the General Hospital. Ariane had insisted on coming. "I don't want to fight with your sister anymore," she said. "I've got bigger things to worry about. And you two should totally make up. You're lucky to have each other."

"I used to think so," Wally said. "Recently, I'm not so sure." But he was secretly glad Ariane had agreed to come.

They took Wally's backpack and another one filled with some of Flish's old clothes that would fit Ariane, including a swimsuit. "We may have to materialize in a swimming pool again," she'd said. "Easier to get away with it if you don't look like you've fallen in."

"You'll still be in the swimming pool with a backpack," Wally pointed out.

"Easier to explain than being fully clothed." She gave him a wicked smile. "Or in your underwear."

"You're never going to let me live that down, are you?"

Her smile widened. "Nope."

As they approached Flish's room they heard a man's voice. For a second, Wally thought it must be a doctor... but then he recognized it. He and Ariane stopped dead at the same instant, and exchanged startled looks. "Rex Major?" Wally whispered, and Ariane nodded. "What's he doing here?"

"Talking to your sister," Ariane said grimly. "Maybe he's planning to take her hostage next."

"Crap," Wally muttered, and hurried forward.

They came around the edge of the door just in time to see Flish stand up and half-fall against Major. She saw them, and gave them a grin that would have looked at home on a shark. Major turned and saw them, too. "Hello, Wally, Ariane," he said. "Nice of you to visit."

Wally felt his hands clench into fists as anger surged through him and he took a step forward. Let the shards take over now if they wanted. He'd gladly stick a knife in Rex Major...

But the shards remained quiescent. The anger was all his. And he couldn't *really* attack Major in the middle of the Regina General Hospital. He let his fists relax. "What are you doing here?" he snarled.

"I just healed your sister's leg," Major said. "Magic can be used for more than hurting people. I told you that. I thought you'd agreed with me." He shook his head. "You've really disappointed me, Wally."

"Boo-hoo," Wally said. He stared at Flish. "Is that true? He fixed your leg?"

"I'm standing, aren't I?" Flish said.

"Felicia," Major said, "is going to come live with me in Toronto. She'll have the life I offered you."

"She's not doing anything of the sort!" Wally snapped. His fists clenched again. "Take her hands off her, or I'll..."

"What? Beat me? Hit me with a poker like you did my

poor guard?" Major smirked. "You'd find that harder than you think. You cannot draw on the shards' power to attack me while I carry one of the shards myself. And I am more than a match for you without that." He put his arm around Flish's shoulder, who smiled smugly. "Felicia has agreed. Your parents have agreed. You really have no say in it, Wally. Now if you'll excuse us, I believe we need to find a doctor to examine Felicia and confirm she is well enough to leave the hospital."

He walked forward, passing Wally without another glance. Flish brushed past him with a nasty grin.

But Ariane, standing behind him, blocked their way. "You're beaten," she told Major. "I have two shards. You have one. I'll hear the song of the fourth shard soon. I can draw on the power of the shards and you can't."

"Can't I?" Major said softly. He regarded her for a moment. "Are you going to let us pass, or do I call security?"

Ariane stared at him, her eyes cold. "You don't have a hostage anymore. Unless that's what Flish is."

"Felicia is my guest, not a hostage," Major said. "She'd hardly work as a hostage when you've already tried to kill her yourself."

"She's Wally sister."

"Well, you almost killed him once, too. Now will you let us pass?"

Lips pressed tight, Ariane stepped to one side. Major went into the hallway and turned back to wait for Flish. But she'd stopped to confront Ariane. Face just inches from the other girl's, she said in a poisonous whisper, "I promised you I'd make you pay for everything you've done. And I will. Don't ever think I won't."

"Follow your master like an obedient bitch, why don't you?" Ariane said levelly.

Flish tensed, and for a moment, Wally thought she would hit Ariane. But then she relaxed. "Your time will come," she said. "Oh, it will definitely come." She went out to Major.

From the hallway, he looked back at Ariane. "As far as hostages go," he said, "don't think for one moment I have exhausted the possibilities. You'll be hearing from me." And then he was gone, Flish walking behind him as though her leg had never been broken.

Wally walked over to the bed and fingered the shattered remains of the cast. "How did he do that?" he said angrily. "He's never shown that kind of magic to us before. Why is he getting stronger?"

Ariane shook her head. "It's the shards," she said. "I guess. More of them found, more magic leaking out for him to use."

Wally turned to her. "Unless it's Flish."

She blinked. "Flish?"

"Think about it," Wally said. "When I touch the shard at the same time as you, your power increases. What if she can do that trick, too? We're brother and sister. If I'm some kind of heir of King Arthur, maybe she is, too."

Ariane groaned. "Oh, no."

"Maybe I'm wrong," Wally said, but he was very much afraid he wasn't.

"Maybe," Ariane said, but it didn't really sound as though she believed that, either. "What did he mean about other hostages?"

Wally had a sinking feeling he knew exactly what he meant. "There's something I haven't told you," he said. "When I had access to Major's computer, I...found something. A picture."

She looked at him expectantly.

"It was of a woman, at a convenience store in Carlyle. Taken a few weeks ago. You couldn't see her very clearly, but someone had labelled it. Major is convinced...it was your mother."

Ariane's face went pale. She put out a hand to clutch the doorjamb. "Mom? She's alive?"

"Major thinks so," Wally said. "That was all he had, that picture. But if he's found something else…" his voice trailed off.

"He's after Mom," Ariane said. "He'll take her prisoner like he did Aunt Phyllis. And this time he won't make any mistakes." She stared at him, eyes haunted. "Wally, if he gets Mom, I'll give him *everything*. Every shard. I'll do *anything* to get her back. You understand that, don't you?"

"I do," Wally said quietly. "But will the shards let you?"

"I control the sword, it doesn't control me," Ariane said. It had the sound of something she'd said often to herself, but it lacked conviction. Then her voice changed, became harder and angrier. "And you took this long to tell me this because…?"

"We were busy," Wally said. "Surviving and travelling and beating Rex Major and stuff like that. I just…forgot." It sounded lame, but it was the truth.

For a moment Ariane's anger remained visible on her face, but then she took a deep breath and the tension vanished. "The picture was weeks old, you said. So I guess it didn't matter much. But Wally…we have to find her. Even while we're looking for the fourth shard, *we have to find my Mom.*"

"Absolutely," Wally said.

"Does Aunt Phyllis know?"

Wally nodded.

"Good." Ariane straightened, took another deep breath. "We'd better go get her. We're going to have to figure out a safe place for her to stay, somewhere Rex Major can't track her to." She opened her backpack, and took out the old swimsuit of Flish's. "Swimming pool time," she said.

"We're going to change here?" Wally said in alarm.

"Where else? I'll go in here," she indicated the bathroom, "and you can pull the curtain and change by the bed. When you're ready come into the bathroom and we'll use the taps to escape."

This is the weirdest thing I've ever done, Wally thought a few moments later as he stripped behind the curtain and then pulled on the trunks he'd packed in his backpack. He stuffed his clothes into the pack and stepped out from behind the curtain.

A nurse had just come into the room. *Of course there'd be a nurse*, Wally thought with resignation. *That's the way my life works.* She stared at him. "Why are you wearing swimming trunks in the hospital? And where's the patient?"

"Talk to the doctor," Wally said. "He'll...explain everything."

"He may know where the patient went," the nurse said, "but I'll be really interested to hear his explanation for *you*." Her expression hardened. "Get dressed and get out of here or I'm calling security."

"I've just...got to use the bathroom first," Wally said, and padded over to it, bare feet cold on the tiles. He opened the door, slipped inside, and closed it behind him.

Ariane was wearing a bikini he remembered his sister wearing a couple of years earlier. He tried not to stare, but it was a tight fit and she was *right there*, and the mirror gave him a view of the other side of her. "Nurse," he squeaked. "In room."

Ariane sighed. "Pull yourself together. It's just skin." She turned to the taps and started the water running. "Let's go."

And just like that, they went.

◄◄ ►►

Ariane had no trouble finding a route to Estevan. She'd been to the smaller city a couple of times and had even gone water-sliding at the Estevan Leisure Centre. She brought them in underwater in the deepest part of the pool and they swam to the surface. *Wally no longer has any problem in the water*, she thought. *He's way better than he should be from just having a couple of lessons. That swim to the island in Lake Putahi...I wonder if that's from the shards, too?*

They attracted a couple of puzzled looks from swimmers who obviously found it peculiar two people had just emerged from a pool they hadn't seen them enter. The looks grew more puzzled as they slung the backpacks out onto the edge of the pool and clambered out themselves. Ariane touched the backpacks, sending the water spraying off of them – and what *that* looked like to the swimmers, she had no idea – then she and Wally went off to their respective change rooms, emerging fully dressed a few minutes later.

Wally had money and the address Aunt Phyllis was staying at, so they called a taxi and rode there in style.

Ariane knocked on the door of the modest bungalow. An elderly woman, surprisingly tall and rather gaunt, answered. She looked down at Ariane, puzzled. "Yes?"

"Is Aunt...is Phyllis Forsythe here?" Ariane said.

The woman's eyes widened. "Oh, my! You must be... Phyllis!" she called over her shoulder. "Phyllis! It's your niece and her boyfriend."

"He's not my –"Ariane began, but the woman had already disappeared.

And then, there was Aunt Phyllis.

She looked the same as always. But then, she'd also looked the same as always the last time Ariane had seen her, when she'd been living in a dream world under Merlin's Command. This time, though, the joy that lit her face on seeing Ariane was one hundred per cent her.

Ariane burst into tears and ran to her.

Aunt Phyllis enveloped her in a deep, comforting hug. "There, there, sweetie," she whispered. "It's all right now. Everything is all right now."

Ariane desperately wanted to believe her, wanted to believe that now they were together again they had nothing else to fear. She wanted to go back home to Regina, back to poor Pendragon, left alone in the house and being looked after by the neighbour, back to her room, even back to the hated Oscana Collegiate. But it wasn't going to happen. None of it. Everything was *not* all right now. Everything would not be all right until she'd seen the Lady's quest through to the end.

And so, much sooner than she wanted, she pushed herself away from Aunt Phyllis. "We've got a lot to tell you, Aunt Phyllis," she said. "And then we've got to leave."

"Leave?" said the gaunt woman.

"Oh!" Aunt Phyllis said. "Where are my manners? Emma, this is my niece, Ariane. And this is Wally, her –"

"He's not my boyfriend," Ariane said automatically, and then wished she hadn't when she saw Wally's expression. She blinked at him. *Wait*, she thought. *He used to deny it, too. Is he…? Does he feel that way about…?*

Everything he'd done he'd said he'd done to protect her and help her. *Of course*, he felt that way about her. She couldn't believe she hadn't guessed until now.

She felt a sense of alarm. But then a strange sort of… warmth. *Wally Knight is in love with me*, she thought. *And I…*

But she didn't finish that thought. *Later*, she thought. *I'll think about it later.*

"Her friend," Aunt Phyllis finished dryly. "Ariane, honey, I don't understand. Why should I have to leave?"

Ariane glanced at Emma. "It's…complicated."

Aunt Phyllis waved a hand. "Don't worry, I've told Emma everything. She knows all about the shards and Rex Major and the Lady of the Lake."

Ariane blinked at the other woman. "You do?"

"Fascinating story," Emma said placidly. "Of course Phyllis had previously told me her tale of seeing the Lady in Emma Lake all those years ago. I've long wondered if there would be more to it."

"O...kay then," Ariane said. She turned back to Aunt Phyllis. "Let me tell you what's happened..."

◀◀ ▶▶

The tale took awhile to tell, and Emma insisted on making tea before she really began, so they finished almost an hour later sitting at the dining-room table, sipping from beautiful gold-rimmed china cups, so delicate Ariane felt ham-fisted holding one. "You came down here on the bus," Ariane said. "That's too public. Sooner or later, Rex Major will be able to trace you here. And when he does..."

Aunt Phyllis sighed. "He'll take me hostage again. And probably use that...what did you call it? Command?...power of his to make me perfectly all right with it. You're right, dear, we'll have to leave."

"I can take you anywhere," Ariane said. "Where would you like to hide out? Wally tells me Major has unwittingly donated a large sum to your bank account, but if you're going to stay in a hotel, it has to be one that doesn't use a computer system for check-ins."

"There's a lovely bed and breakfast out in the Cypress Hills," Aunt Phyllis said. "I stayed there for a week once. The couple who run it are elderly and old-fashioned. There's no computer access. There's no cell-phone coverage. Just a landline. I would be very happy there. There were some very interesting books in the parlor."

"Is there a pond or lake nearby?"

Aunt Phyllis nodded.

"Then that's our place. Can you call them?"

"I'll make the plans."

"Book for two," Emma said. "I'm coming with you."

"Really, Emma, there's no need –"

"Oh, balderdash. We've seen far too little of each other these past few years. Besides, we can book it in my name and then there's no way any of Rex Major's nasty magic computer fingers can trace it to you."

"Well, I would be glad of the company," Aunt Phyllis said. "Come along, then."

Ariane gaped after them. "Great," she said. "Now I have to take *two* of them."

"*Can* you take two at once?" Wally said.

Ariane thought about it. "I don't think that's a good idea," she said. "Especially not with first-timers. I might manage you and another person, since you're not likely to panic anymore."

"Oh, no, I quite enjoy being dissolved and reconstituted in some random lake or swimming pool," Wally said. "One of my favourite things ever." But he grinned as he said it.

She'd used to think that grin was ugly. Now she found it rather endearing.

"If you can do that," he went on, "can I go with you when you take Aunt Phyllis? I really want to see her reaction at the other end. Especially if you're materializing in a cow pond. And it might make her less scared."

"Sure. But I think she'll be fine with it." Ariane looked out of the dining room toward the hallway where she could hear Emma talking on the phone. "She's a surprising lady."

"Is she a lot like your mother?"

"I didn't used to think so," Ariane said. "Now...I'm kind of hoping so. Because if Mom is like Aunt Phyllis, wherever Mom is, she's doing fine."

"I'm sure she is," Wally said. To her surprise, he reached across the table and took her hands. "And if she's not, you'll rescue her and *make* her fine."

Ariane looked down at the hands holding hers, and felt that strange warmth inside her again. She squeezed. "*We'll* rescue her. From now on, we're in this together."

Smiling the crooked smile she was beginning to love, Wally Knight squeezed her hands back. "That," he said, "suits me fine."

ACKNOWLEDGEMENTS

Thanks first to my terrific editor, Matthew Hughes – who, by the way, is himself a fabulous science fiction and fantasy author. You should read his stuff: www.archonate.com.

Second, thanks to the wonderful folks at Coteau Books for doing such a great job with design, publicity, and promotion. You're the best!

And third, thanks to my wife, Margaret Anne, and daughter, Alice (to both of whom I read this entire book aloud), for being loving, supporting...and putting up with a husband and father who spends his days making up stories.

ABOUT THE AUTHOR

EDWARD WILLETT is the award-winning author of more than fifty science-fiction and fantasy novels, science and other non-fiction books for both young readers and adults, including the acclaimed fantasy series *The Masks of Aygrima*, written under the pen name E.C. Blake.

His science fiction novels include *Lost in Translation, Marseguro* and *Terra Insegura. Marseguro* won the 2009 Prix Aurora Award for best Canadian science-fiction and fantasy novel.

His non-fiction writing for young readers has received National Science Teachers Association and VOYA awards.

Edward Willett was born in New Mexico and grew up in Weyburn, Sask. He has lived and worked in Regina since 1988. In addition to his numerous writing projects, Edward is also a professional actor and singer who has performed in dozens of plays, musicals and operas in and around Saskatchewan, hosted local television programs and emceed numerous public events.

BOOKS IN

THE SHARDS OF EXCALIBUR

SERIES:

Book One
Song of the Sword

Book Two
Twist of the Blade

Book Three
The Lake in the Clouds

COMING IN FALL 2015:

The Cave Beneath the Sea

Book Four in
The Shards of Excalibur
series